Mysteries Beneath the Inn

A Maddie Brooke Mystery

Nancy M. Wade

Published in the United States

GARNAN Enterprises, LLC of Ohio.

Copyright 2024 by Nancy M. Wade

All Rights Reserved.

ISBN: 979-89919301-09

ISBN: E979-89919301-16

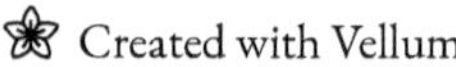 Created with Vellum

Also By: Nancy M. Wade

A Maddie Brooke Mystery

- **Innvitation to Murder**
- **Mysteries Beneath the Inn**

A Meadowood Mystery

- **Scarecrows and Corpses**
- **Deadly Bones**
- **Reunion With Death**
- **Deathly Wedding Woes**
- **Berry Little Murder**
- **Deadly Secrets**

Circle-D Saga Trilogy

- **Endless Circle**
- **Moment In Time**
- **Gun For Hire**

MYSTERIES BENEATH THE INN

Nancy M. Wade

Contents

Cast of Characters

- **Polly A. (nee Stewart) Brooke** – Grannie, resident ghost, married Charles Brooke with Southern roots dating back before the Civil War.
- **Madison Leigh Brooke (Maddie)**- 23 year-old granddaughter of Polly, graduate of UVA in Charlottesville, a history major with a nose for research and investigation.
- **Thomas Borden** – long-time employee of the Magnolia Blossom B&B; he is chef and handyman at the inn.
- **Detective Allen Crawford** – a Philadelphia Yankee who's joined the Charlottesville police force; he solves crime while dazzling the local female population; cousin to the groom
- **Lionel Hogan** – Maddie's school friend. Lionel is a wiz with computers; works as an I.T. forensic security analyst.
- **Dr. Lily Chung** – Maddie's former roommate at UVA, Lily is an intern at the UVA Medical Center
- **Savannah Collier** – bride, hot-tempered red head
- **Stephen Beauregard** – groom, a Rhett Butler look alike
- **James Warner** – bestman, friend of Stephen and a con man

- **Susan Harper** — maid of honor, Savannah's friend but secretly covets the groom
- **Stanton and Martha Collier** — nouveau riche, desire a place in Southern high society
- **Hugh and Beatrice Beauregard** — old Southern aristocratic family with more charm than money
- **Sally Rawlins** — live-in housekeeper at the inn, recent widow
- **Dr. Wilbur Houser** — local country doctor
- **Carl Harding** — brother of Susan Harper
- **Reverend Jacob Moore** — officiate wedding ceremony
- **Chief Bill Barlow** — runs the detective division of Charlottesville PD; resents Crawford as a know it all Yankee
- **Prissy** - the Inn's black and white tuxedo cat
- **Luke** — Grannie's protective German shepherd
- **Folks of Clarkstown**

Chapter One

Curses

The sweet scent of magnolia blossoms drifted on the late morning breeze, mingling with the fresh tang of succulent apples ready to harvest from the adjacent orchard. Chickens clucked in their nearby roost and the black and white tuxedo cat, Prissy, marched her latest litter of kittens across the yard. Surveying my realm, I stood on the wide wraparound porch that hugged the centuries-old farmhouse like a warm embrace.

Magnolia Blossom Inn existed in a converted pre-Civil War era farmhouse that the Brooke family had built and lived in since 1830, passed down from one generation to another. I grew up in this old house and on the farm with its cherry and apple orchards. When my mother died, I was only seven years old. My father, a sea captain, brought me to live with his parents: Charles and Polly Brooke. My father preferred life at sea to raising a lone daughter, so the task fell to my loving grandparents. Every so many years, he'd stop by to visit. The last time I saw my father it was at Grannie's funeral. He went back to his cargo ships and now I was truly on my own. Well, maybe not completely. I should have known that Grannie would never abandon me as he did.

Growing up on the farm, all its rich history engulfed me and inspired my imagination and love of all things historical, especially pertaining to the colonial time period. I suppose that's why I got my degree in American history from the University of Virginia.

Located within an easy commute to the city of Charlottesville, the inn was an ideal location for tourists wanting a quiet spot to stay but close enough to nearby historical attractions like Monticello. Magnolia Blossom Inn offered five bedrooms with private baths for guests and two bedrooms on the third floor with a shared bath for the owners. The large comfortable living room with a brick hearth opened into a formal dining room where guests enjoyed a daily sumptuous breakfast.

A light breeze ruffled my long hair. The pleasant temperature felt just right, making it perfect summer weather for a wedding. Delicate meadow flowers waved their colorful heads at the entrance to the orchard, Grannie's favorite flowers—vibrant and natural. Gazing out at the Blue Ridge Mountains that rose majestically a short distance from Magnolia Blossom Inn, my mind mulled over a thousand worries.

A mug of coffee in one hand, a sense of anticipation buzzed through me. This place was mine now—to build and grow into a prosperous business as I hoped or risk losing to disaster and financial ruin if my expansion plans fell flat. I was gambling with my future. It was a daunting prospect to someone who had just graduated from college a little over a year ago. Taking a deep breath, I tried to ignore the growing sense of dread in my chest.

It wasn't just the upcoming wedding that had me on edge, it was the sense that something else was coming, something darker—something my ghostly grandmother had been hinting at all day.

"You feel it too, don't you?" I muttered under my breath.

A faint, disembodied chuckle answered me. *"Well, sugar, if you didn't feel it, I'd wonder if you were even my granddaughter."*

I rolled my eyes, though I couldn't suppress the grin that followed. Talking to Grannie's ghost had become as normal as my morning coffee—except when it came with ominous warnings.

"You're not exactly filling me with confidence, Grannie."

Luke, my German shepherd dog, relaxed in the warm July sunshine heating the porch floorboards. The kitchen screen door slammed behind him and he barked in greeting as Lionel joined us.

"Maddie, darling, we've got an issue. The wedding planner is having a meltdown and Savannah is turning into a bridezilla."

"Oh no! What now? Good gracious, the wedding is just hours away."

"I dunno. Something about bourbon and curses."

Lionel, my best friend and resident computer tech wizard, sauntered up with his tablet in hand. He looked dapper in his skinny jeans and pastel lavender polo accenting his ebony skin, a fashion style only Lionel could wear. "Has Grannie been by yet this morning?"

I gave him a playful nudge. "No Grannie sightings yet, but I've heard her voice."

Lionel raised an eyebrow. "Maybe she's hiding and is really the one behind this curse."

"Don't be disrespectful. She's probably just waiting for the right moment to startle me." I laughed, thinking of Grannie's mischievous spirit that had a way of popping up when I least expected. Ever since she passed a year ago and I inherited the inn, her ghost had been hanging around—giving advice, rolling her eyes at my choices, and occasionally spooking the guests. I wouldn't trade peace and calm over her mischievous spirit for anything.

Originally, only Luke and I could see and hear Grannie, but after a lot of soul searching and discussion, Grannie materialized and showed herself to both of my friends. Lily, with her Chinese ancestry and physician's experience of strong lingering life forces, took it in stride and accepted the phenomenon. Lionel's more analytical mind took some time to convince, and it was harder for him to accept the possibility. I think Grannie knew how much I relied upon my friends' counsel and that it would help me if they could also see her and, therefore, wouldn't doubt my sanity.

Across the yard, Dr. Lily Chung emerged from the barn with her stethoscope slung around her neck, looking like a city doctor plopped in the middle of a country postcard. Lily and I had shared a dorm room as undergraduates at the University of Virginia, Charlottesville. Upon graduation, our careers took different paths but our friendship remained solid. She gave us a wave as she made her way over, her scrubs and clogs dusted from the gravel yard.

"Good morning, y'all!" she called, flashing her usual bright smile. "The barn looks marvelous. I just had to come early and take a peek. I love the deep rose color the bride chose for the linens and streamers. You guys ready for the big wedding occasion?"

"Oh, we're ready," I said, taking a sip of my coffee. "I just hope everything goes off without a hitch.

"And your first bridal party murder," came a raspy, Southern voice from behind me. I didn't even have to turn around to know it was Grannie. *"You always did like a challenge, baby girl."*

I sighed and turned, but, as usual, there was no sign of her. Just her words hanging in the air like an ominous cloud.

"Maddie," Lionel said, his eyes wide, "Did she just—"

"Yes, she did," I muttered, my stomach flipping at the thought. My grandmother was rarely wrong about anything, even from beyond the grave, but I sincerely prayed her prediction was mistaken this time.

Before I could think too much about it, the crunch of gravel pulled my attention to the driveway. A dark sedan came into view, and out stepped handsome Detective Allen Crawford. A northern transplant to the Charlottesville police department, Allen had charmed the local feminine population with his dark good looks and reserved manner, enough to make them forget he was a dreaded Philadelphia Yankee. My heart skipped a beat every time he showed up. We had shared more than a few sparks during our past involvement in Grannie's death and the last big murder case at the inn. But this wasn't the time to worry about my complicated feelings toward the man.

"What's he doing here?" I whispered to Lionel.

"Apparently, he's the groom's cousin. Didn't you know?"

Allen smiled when he saw me, his gold-flecked hazel eyes catching mine. "Morning, Maddie. Hope I'm not interrupting."

"Never," I said, trying not to sound too flustered. My fingers unconsciously twirled a lock of hair as I averted my eyes from his penetrating hazel ones. "We were just discussing the upcoming wedding ceremony. You're a few hours early if you're attending as a guest."

"When I heard the wedding was at Magnolia Blossom this weekend, naturally, I begged for an invitation," he said, stepping up onto the porch with a grin. "Thought I'd drop by early and make sure everything's under control. Seriously ... is there anything I can do to help?"

"Everything's just fine," I said, though Grannie's cryptic message still echoed in my head.

Lionel leaned over, whispering in my ear. "Considering what Grannie's been whispering about all day, I'd say he's here just in time for whatever disaster's about to strike."

Grannie floated over, casting an amused glance at Lionel. *"He's not wrong. That young man's gonna need all the help he can get—and so are you."*

I sighed and ran a hand through my blond hair. With an aside to Lionel, I mumbled, "Great. Just what I needed. A wedding on the verge of collapse, a detective with family ties, and the looming sense that someone's about to turn up dead."

As if on cue, the sound of raised voices drifted across the porch. I exchanged a look with Lily and Lionel, who both raised an eyebrow in silent question. We headed toward the commotion.

Grannie floated along behind us, muttering, *"Told you so."*

Inside the formal dining room, chaos reigned. The wedding planner, a small but fiery woman named Darcy, was waving her arms wildly as she argued with the bride. Savannah, a lovely but hot-tempered red head, looked about five seconds from breaking into tears. Parents and bridal party members crowded the room.

"I don't care if it's tradition!" Savannah shouted, her Southern accent thickening with each word. "I'm not letting that cursed bottle near my wedding!" She stomped her foot to emphasize her demand.

Darcy sighed, exasperated.

"Savannah, honey, it's part of our family history! The Beauregard family has been serving that bourbon at every wedding for generations." Stephen Beauregard, with his dark Rhett Butler looks, tried to soothe his angry bride-to-be as he wrapped his arms around her. He pressed a kiss against her cheek. Savannah was having none of it and pushed him away.

I entered the room and stood next to the polished mahogany buffet that stood against one wall holding a silver tea service. From my position, I could observe everyone's actions. The bride's parents, Martha and Stanton Collier, perched on Chippendale chairs along one side of the long antique dining table. Remnants of the elaborate breakfast they had consumed still clung to plates and bowls on the table. I spotted Tom waiting awkwardly in the kitchen doorway, wanting to get in to clear the table, but not wanting to interrupt the private discussion.

Hugh Beauregard occupied the head of the table with a stern look on his face. His timid wife, Beatrice, wrung her hands and wisely stayed silent. I spotted the best man and maid of honor hovering near their friends, ready to step in and defend each sparring partner as needed. Lionel and Lily crowded in beside me. Allen Crawford watched the scene with his arms crossed, his jaw set in a determined way that I recognized all too well. I glanced between him and the groom; I could see the family resemblance despite Allen's beard.

Savannah perked up when she saw me.

"Maddie, thank goodness you're here! Please tell Darcy and Stephen we don't need to use that ridiculous bourbon bottle at my wedding. I want nothing cursed happening on my big day."

I frowned, casting a glance at Lionel, who just gave me a look that said, 'This is your mess, not mine.'

"Cursed?" I asked, trying to stay neutral.

Savannah nodded, her pale eyes wide. "It's been in the Beauregard family for ages, but every time it's used, something awful happens. That bottle is bad luck, and I'm not about to take any chances at my wedding."

"That's ridiculous! There's no such curse," Hugh Beauregard shouted and stormed out of the room, pushing past me. His wife meekly followed in his wake.

"Sugar, if you don't want the disgusting bourbon, then we won't have it. My princess can have whatever she wants," cajoled Stanton Collier and with that said, he rose and left the room.

His wife appeared uncertain but stayed behind and poured herself a cup of tea from the sideboard.

"Don't go and get yourself all upset, dear. We need to dress for the wedding soon. You don't want to appear all flushed," her mother cautioned.

"Maybe you can just pour a glass of the bourbon to be used as a toast at the reception," I suggested. "You don't have to have the bottle on the table; we can dispense the shots in the kitchen."

"Yeah, I guess," Stephen said, agreeing to the compromise.

"C'mon buddy, I've got something to discuss with you," James Warner, the best man, said as he pulled on Stephen's arm.

The groom appeared hesitant to leave Savannah's side. I could see him wavering between consoling his sweetheart or escaping with his friend. He wisely chose to stay after reading the expression and warning glint in Savannah's eyes. Warner shrugged and departed the room alone.

Darcy exited through the swinging doors into our kitchen and I assumed she took the disputed bottle with her because it was gone from the table.

Allen nodded to me, a smile of approval on his face for my diplomatic solution. Disaster averted. Or was it?

The photographer posed the bride and groom under the floral archway. Savannah glowed like a Southern princess. A radiant bride with silky auburn hair cascading in curls down her back, complimenting her peaches and cream complexion. Her bridal gown hugged her curves then flowed around her in a silken cloud. She held a bouquet of white magnolia blossoms, fuchsia peonies, white roses, and baby breath. Next to her stood the proud groom. If anyone portrayed an image of a perfect Southern gentleman planter, it was Stephen Beauregard. With his dark hair, thin mustache, and fitted tuxedo, he appeared to have stepped out of Gone With The Wind. As a bridal couple, they were more attractive than the plastic pair sitting on top of the wedding cake.

The couple returned to the wide veranda of the inn and posed in different positions with the magnolia trees as their backdrop. Some people would frown and worry that it was bad luck to see the bride before the ceremony, but Savannah had dismissed that idea. She insisted on their formal portraits to be taken before the ceremony and guest arrivals. I couldn't help but wonder at her earlier claim about a cursed bottle of bourbon, yet she easily ignored the traditional superstitions. I don't know whether she had taken a valium or perhaps had sipped some of that bourbon but her calm demeanor showed a 360 degree turn-around. While she smiled and flirted with the groom, the rest of us waited until it was time for the nuptials to begin.

Allen had changed into his formal attire. He made quite the feast for my hungry eyes; his animal magnetism sparking each time I looked his way. He smiled at me knowingly and I felt my cheeks grow warm. Good gracious, was I that obvious? I turned away from him and smoothed my pale blue gown.

Lily and Lionel, both looking cute in their server uniforms, joined me in the dining room as I arranged platters of cookies to be later carried out to the barn with the dessert trays and wedding cake. Coming up behind me, Allen reached for one of the sugary treats and I raised an eyebrow at his sweet tooth.

"What? One cookie won't hurt," he said as he ate it in two bites.

"I'm hungry. I skipped lunch to get here early. I'm looking forward to dinner."

We both jumped when a loud shot rang out.

"Was that—?" Lionel started.

"I think it was."

Allen's expression shifted instantly to that of a detective on alert. "That sounded serious."

I nodded, dread filling my stomach. "Sounded like that came from the banquet barn," I answered, already moving toward the kitchen door. Lionel and Lily were close on my heels. Allen had run two steps ahead of me. Savannah lifted the hem of her gown, and with Stephen, rushed across the porch and ran toward the barn.

When we reached the barn doors, I threw them open, my heart pounding in my chest. There, in the middle of the rustic space where the wedding reception was supposed to take place, lay a man—his body twisted unnaturally. On the floor, amidst a pool of spilled whiskey and shards of broken glass, his blood mixed with the amber liquid. A wisp of smoke and the scent of gunpowder hung in the air.

Grannie's ghost floated closer, her voice tight. *"Oh, sugar. This is bad ... that's Savannah's father."*

Savannah and Stephen both charged into the barn. Savannah screamed at the sight of her father. Stephen clutched her to him, burying her face in his solid chest and turned her away from the gruesome sight.

"Dear Lord," Lily whispered, as she crouched down beside the body, her physician's fingers going to the man's neck, searching for a pulse. She shook her head no.

A quick glance around revealed the shattered remains of the very bourbon bottle Savannah had been arguing about hours ago.

"Savannah was right. That bottle might really be cursed," I mumbled.

Allen knelt beside Lily. He carefully rolled the body over; the eyes stared lifelessly at the ceiling. Allen scanned the body for any signs of struggle and clues of the assailant.

He muttered, his voice tense. "A cursed bourbon bottle didn't kill him. But someone did. This man's shot."

Lionel gasped. "Grannie was right," he whispered to me.

I swallowed hard, a mixture of fear and disbelief washing over me. Grannie had warned me.

"Maddie," Allen said, his eyes meeting mine. "This wasn't an accident. We've got a murder on our hands."

He reached for his cell phone and dialed the police station. I heard him ask for the forensics team to come out and realized my lovely wedding venue was now a crime scene.

I stared down at the lifeless body of Stanton Collier, trying to piece together what had just happened. I didn't understand it. Everyone was so happy just the night before at the rehearsal dinner. What was going to happen now? Would there even be a wedding ceremony?

Chapter Two

Rehearsal Dinner

Looking back on that night now, it's hard to believe how everything seemed so perfect—so full of promise and then turned out so wrong. If only I had paid more attention to the subtle cracks beneath the surface.

The Magnolia Blossom Inn glowed in the golden light of sunset, with strings of twinkling lights draped around the barn and the smell of Chef Tom's rosemary-roasted chicken wafting through the air. This was our first big wedding event; Tom and I had pulled out all the stops. Even my friends pitched in to help make the event a success.

We'd spent the past two months renovating the large barn into an attractive venue for weddings and banquets. Tom and I swept clean all traces of farm animals except for a few bales of hay left in the loft to add a rustic touch. A high-rise platform had been constructed to hold musical performers. The barn's concrete flooring had been painted a pewter gray color, and a portable wooden dance floor occupied the center of the room. We grouped round tables, seating six diners each, around the room to accommodate a party size as big as ninety. Long buffet tables sat along one wall, at right angles from the stage. A floral archway stood near the entrance to provide a backdrop for photos. Wide fabric streamers, in the bride's chosen color theme, draped artfully from ceiling beams and matched the table linens. Vases of fresh flowers adorned the center of each table.

"I like what you've done with the place. It'll be fun to witness the parties in this place," Grannie said.

"Don't get any ideas of spooking the bride or groom … they're nervous enough as it is."

"Oh pooh! I'd never! You take all the fun out of being a ghost." With that statement, she disappeared in a poof of cold air.

Shaking my head and swallowing a chuckle at her antics, my eyes roamed the horizon, taking in the cherry and apple orchards, the farm's buildings, and newly renovated barn.

I had invested a good sum of money, time, and effort to transform the barn into a revenue-making enterprise to add financial support to the inn. Reservations at the inn provided daily operating money but I needed more substantial funding for updates to the historic building.

There was a lot riding on this wedding. I'd been so focused on making everything flawless that I hadn't noticed the undercurrents of tension among the wedding party swirling just beneath the surface.

I observed the wedding group from the house veranda. They were a curious bunch. The bride, Savannah Collier, floated between guests, her ivory rehearsal dress catching the light as she flashed a radiant smile at everyone she passed. She was young, beautiful, and giddy with excitement. The bride was also used to getting her way from her indulgent parents. Martha and Stanton Collier beamed with pride, clearly eager to cement their place in local society with their daughter's prominent wedding.

Martha, a petite woman with perfectly coiffed hair, had stood by my side earlier, fanning herself in the early evening heat, whispering, "You know, Maddie, we're just so thrilled to be here. This wedding is going to put our name in the society pages of the Charlottesville Gazette."

I nodded politely, even though I knew exactly what she meant. The Colliers were nouveau riche, having struck it rich in some tech investment a few years back, or so the story goes. I didn't understand all the complexities of Collier's business but I was sure Lionel would. They were desperate to be accepted by the old, established Southern vanguard, like the Beauregards.

The Beauregards, meanwhile, were doing everything they could to hide the fact that their pristine Southern manners were all they had left, their bank accounts sorely wanting. Anyone from the county knew the truth; only newcomers like the Colliers were taken in by the phony polished charm. Beatrice Beauregard, Savannah's future mother-in-law, had positioned herself near the head of the banquet table, giving out polite smiles and sipping sweet tea, while her husband, Hugh, was busy laughing a little too loudly at every joke Stanton made.

"Now, Stanton," Hugh boomed, slapping the other man on the back with just a hint of desperation in his voice. "We need to talk after dinner. I have a little … proposition that could benefit us both."

I caught the look in Stanton's eyes—a mixture of curiosity and suspicion—and knew right away that whatever Hugh was planning, it had everything to do with the Collier money. Maybe he wasn't as gullible as I had thought.

The tension between the families wasn't the only thing swirling around that night. Savannah's maid of honor, Susan Harper, had been oddly quiet during the entire event. Studying her, I thought her smile a bit forced. If these two women were close friends, they didn't act like it. She sat to the side, watching Savannah with an expression that seemed supportive on the surface, but there was something about her eyes … a hunger, maybe. I saw it when she looked at Stephen Beauregard, the groom-to-be, and I knew right then and there that Susan's "support" was anything but genuine while she coveted her friend's man.

She wasn't the only one with secrets.

James Warner, the best man and Stephen's old college buddy, seemed to spend the entire night chatting up Stanton Collier. I didn't think much of it at the time—just another businessman trying to impress the big spender in the room. But there was something off about

James, as if he wasn't fully committed to the role he assumed. He played on Stanton's interest in Civil War history and flattered the older man in an obvious ploy. James' talk of *"hidden Confederate treasures"* and *"getting in on a once-in-a-lifetime opportunity"* made my skin crawl. I wasn't sure whether it was the alcohol talking or something more sinister. I just knew I didn't like the man.

"Maddie! Where are you? Everything is going perfectly," Lionel called, waving from across the lawn as he chatted with a few of the guests outside the barn. He looked stylish as always, his smile infectious, but even he couldn't see the subtle tensions threading through the evening.

"Coming!" I called back, smoothing my dress and trying to push down the nagging feeling in the back of my mind.

I made my way through the gathering, exchanging polite smiles and checking in on the guests. Tom had outdone himself with the menu— roasted chicken plus a perfectly seared beef tenderloin, local vegetables roasted to perfection, and a dessert that was certain to tempt everyone. Judging by this delicious offering for the rehearsal dinner, the wedding fare promised to be spectacular.

Tom was the real treasure that kept guests coming back to the inn. Thomas Borden started work at Magnolia Blossom when my Grand-daddy, Charles Brooke, was still alive sixteen years ago. He wore dual hats of cook and maintenance man around the inn with his delicious gourmet breakfasts that guests enjoyed. He was a culinary genius. Tom was quiet and unassuming and very gracious to the folks staying at the inn. I depended upon his easy manner and competence to help me manage the business. He was like the older brother I never had.

"Maddie," Lily said as she pulled me aside. "You're going to be booked out for years after this wedding. Everything looks amazing."

Her voice was full of pride, but I couldn't shake the feeling that something was ... off.

I smiled and squeezed her hand, grateful for her friendship. "I hope so. This could really put Magnolia Blossom on the map. I can't thank you enough for sacrificing your weekend off from the hospital to lend a hand here. A huge reception is just too much for Sally. Once I find some reliable local help that can be hired for special occasions, things will run smoother."

We both glanced over at the families seated around the banquet table positioned in the center of the barn. Savannah laughed with her mother and the groom. Stanton leaned in to whisper something to James Warner. I saw Hugh Beauregard's eyes darting around as if he were already counting the money in his head. Susan sat silently observing them all.

That's when I noticed Grannie hovering by the barn doors, her figure flickering in the dim light. She was watching the rehearsal dinner unfold with that familiar look of hers, the one that said she knew something I didn't.

"What is it, Grannie?" I whispered under my breath, but she vanished before I could get any closer.

Now, as I sat here in the quiet aftermath of what had happened, the laughter and smiles of that night faded like a distant dream. Who knew that by the next morning, Stanton Collier would be dead—shot in the very barn where we had celebrated just hours before?

My thoughts drifted back to the night of the rehearsal dinner, to every subtle glance, every whispered conversation. What had I missed? Who had been plotting all along, right under my nose?

Allen walked up beside me, his presence both comforting and unnerving. "You looked like you were a million miles away," he said softly.

"I was," I replied. "Thinking about last night ... and how everything had seemed so perfect."

He sighed, his eyes scanning the now-empty barn. "Well, it wasn't. Someone had planned a much different outcome."

I nodded, the pit in my stomach growing heavier.

"Poor Martha. The Collier name will certainly be in the Gazette now, but not how she envisioned."

"No doubt, reporters will play this up for all it's worth."

I watched Luke prowling around the yard, losing sight of him as he trotted into the orchard. My thoughts kept returning to the dead body we found lying in the barn.

"Can you stay over? I've got one empty room. I'd feel better if you were on premises. It frightens me to think that among these people staying in my house, one of them is a murderer."

"Yeah, I'll stay. I want to investigate the scene some more," Allen replied. "Where is everyone now?"

"Sheltering in their rooms. Chief Barlow told everyone to stay in place until you release the crime scene. Does this mean the wedding ceremony must be called off?" I asked.

"Hmm, for the time being. Like you said, it's a crime scene."

I rose from the porch swing and turned to go inside when I heard Luke barking insistently. His loud barking came from the apple orchard. Luke only sounded like that when he detected danger or when someone put him in a threatening posture.

I shot a worried look at Allen as we both ran down the porch steps.

Good gracious! Now what?!

Chapter Three

Pistols

Luke continued barking and growling as he pawed at the ground around the base of a young apple tree. Allen and I hurried into the orchard toward the big German shepherd.

"Luke, heel. Come here boy," I commanded and clapped my hands. The dog barked then obeyed and came to my side. Dirt covered his paws and muzzle.

"What did you find? What is it, boy?" Allen asked as he patted the big dog on his side then stooped and raked the ground with his hands.

Luke had dug a small hole; piles of soil were strewn about as if he had uncovered a favorite bone. To my shock, something far different came into view. A pistol lay buried under the dirt, its grip protruded upward. Allen pulled a hanky from his pocket and reached for the weapon. He stood and held the antique Civil War revolver between thumb and forefinger.

"Well, what do we have here?" mumbled Allen as he turned the gun over and examined it.

"My goodness. Do you think someone buried that gun over a hundred years ago?" I stared at the antique gun.

Allen snorted. "Hardly. Look how shallow that hole is. Luke was easily able to uncover it with his paws. See how fresh the dirt looks? If that gun had been buried since the Civil War, it would have been in the ground much deeper. This gun is too clean. Looks like someone hastily buried this weapon. Maybe Luke interrupted the killer hiding the gun. No, I'd say once I have this tested, we may have found the murder weapon of Stanton Collier."

A memory popped into my head.

"Hmm, I wonder? Come into the house with me. My granddaddy owned a collection of antique firearms. I haven't looked in that case in a while but it's possible that gun may be his."

Allen followed me back to the house. I paused on the back porch and considered Luke's soiled feet.

"Whoa, you're not tracking that mess onto my clean floors. You stay out here until I can wash you up."

Luke whimpered. He understood my words as he tilted his head sideways, gave me a pitiful look, then lay down on the porch. I patted the top of his head before entering the kitchen behind Allen.

"This way, down the hall in the study," I directed.

I opened the door to the small study lined with bookshelves and knotty-pine paneling. A pair of comfortable chairs sat next to a small desk where Grannie used to do her correspondence and where I now take care of inn business. The last time I had been in this room with Allen, he had saved my life. Shaking off that dark memory, I moved to the wooden case in the corner, with its glass door, displaying my granddaddy's collection.

Allen lifted the hinged case lid. A vacant space stood out against the red velvet lining. Each weapon rested in the case with a small identifying tag next to it. Granddaddy Charles had proudly displayed his snub-nosed derringer with its ivory handle and a blunt pepperbox pistol. He also owned an 1860 Colt Army revolver, an antique flintlock, and according to the name tag ... a Remington Army revolver. The Remington now rested in Allen's palm.

"Who had access to this case? Was it usually locked?" Allen asked.

"The lid has a small lock but the key is kept in a tray in my center desk drawer. Normally the study is off limits to guests. I prefer to keep it private so I can conduct the inn's business. I hate to admit it, but when Savannah and her parents arrived two days ago, I did ask Tom to show Mr. Collier the gun collection. He had professed to being an amateur historian of the Civil War era and owned a modest collection of memorabilia. I thought he'd enjoy seeing these. I don't know if Tom or Stanton later showed the collection to the other men. The study door isn't locked. I suppose anyone could have entered the room."

"Do you know if these guns were kept loaded in the case?"

"My granddaddy was old school ... he used to say, *'what good is a gun without bullets'*, so I guess they were. Maybe not the flintlock for obvious reasons, but the others likely have ammunition," I said.

"I'm going to have the gun tested, see if it's been fired recently and if it matches the bullet retrieved from Collier's body. Will you be okay if I'm gone for awhile? I've got to drive back to Charlottesville."

"Of course. I'll be fine. I'll leave the outside light on for you. Sally and Tom are here. Tom agreed to stay late to cook dinner for our guests since they're forbidden to leave," I said.

"I should be back in a couple of hours," Allen said as he wrapped the gun in a cloth napkin and hurried to his car.

The inn had never felt so suffocating. The tension inside was as thick as the humid summer air, hanging heavy in every corner of the house. The once-cheerful wedding guests were now prisoners—bound together not by celebration, but by suspicion. Stanton Collier's murder had turned everything upside down, and the weight of it bore down on me like a lead blanket.

The sun had dipped below the horizon, casting long shadows across the wrap-around porch where I stood, my hands gripping the railing as I stared out at the darkening orchard. Among those trees laden with ripe fruit, someone had discarded an antique revolver in the same callous manner they had discarded the life of Stanton Collier. I shuddered as the reality sunk in.

"Be careful, baby girl, there's foul play in the air," Grannie whispered then vanished from sight.

I tried to take in a deep breath of the cool evening air, but my chest was tight, my mind racing. Inside, the dining room was lit, casting a warm glow through the large windows, but the mood within was anything but warm. A few hours ago, that room had been the heart of a celebration, full of laughter and toasts. Now, it was the epicenter of distrust and volatile emotions.

I heard the low hum of voices from inside, rising and falling, a mix of anger and grief. Savannah's voice broke through the noise, a high, pleading sound that sent a shiver down my spine. She stood with Stephen in the living room, their backs turned away from the others, their heads together in serious discussion. I caught snatches of their conversation.

"... I've spent all afternoon on the phone, calling people, giving excuses. Do you care how humiliated I felt?" Savannah cried.

"What do you want me to do?" Stephen snapped.

Returning to the house, I silently passed by our comfortable living room adorned with a lively plaid sofa in navy blue, yellow, and hunter green on a white backdrop, mirroring the Stewart tartan linked to Grannie's Scottish heritage. The room evoked comfort, relaxation, and invited guests to view the pleasing framed portrayals of a bucolic Virginia countryside or curl up with a book in front of a crackling fire. Now it seemed a place to mourn.

I moved past the doorway, intending to give the couple their privacy. My footsteps tread softly on the hardwood floor as I made my way toward the dining room and kitchen beyond.

The scent of Tom's cooking—something hearty and savory—filled the air, but even his talent couldn't mask the sour taste of fear that permeated the inn. Savannah and Stephen shuffled into the dining room to join the others. I noticed Susan sidled up to Stephen's side and whispered in his ear. Consoling or seducing? I wondered.

The dining room was full. Everyone sat at the long mahogany table, though no one seemed interested in eating. A tear-streaked Martha sat at the head of the table. Savannah plopped down next to her mother. Her eyes shot daggers at her intended groom as she flicked her long red hair off her shoulders.

On the other end of the table sat Beatrice and Hugh, who wore expressions of forced composure—each of them a mask, hiding their true thoughts. Stephen joined his parents as if the two families had retreated into opposing forces. Susan Harper sat quietly next to Savannah, her eyes cast longing glances at Stephen, while James fiddled with his fork. He appeared like a guilty school boy with his hand caught in the cookie jar.

I helped Tom serve the platters of food and made my way around the table pouring glasses of sweet tea or cups of coffee. Normally, I didn't join my guests for meals, but these weren't normal times. Sliding into an empty chair at the side of the table, I tried to be unobtrusive. No one spoke as I sat down, but the tension was palpable. Every eye darted around the table, scanning for signs of guilt.

Martha finally broke the silence, her voice tight and controlled. "We shouldn't be here like this." Her eyes flicked over to Hugh Beauregard. "This ... situation is absurd. We should be mourning Stanton, not sitting here eating like nothing happened. I have funeral arrangements to make."

Hugh raised an eyebrow, his drawl cool and unbothered. "I agree, Martha, but Chief Barlow insists we stay put until the investigation is complete. It's not like we have a choice."

Savannah's voice cracked. "He's right. We have to stay, Mama."

Martha turned sharply to her daughter, her eyes blazing. "Don't you 'he's right' me, Savannah! Your father is dead, and we're sitting here with people who—" She stopped short, swallowing the rest of her words. But we all knew what she meant. Someone in this room might have killed him.

The tension snapped as Stephen slammed his hand on the table. "Enough!" His normally calm, Southern charm had all but disappeared. "This isn't helping anyone."

His mother, Beatrice, laid a hand on his arm, her voice a silky drawl as she spoke. "Stephen, darling, we must stay composed. It's bad manners; we mustn't let our emotions get the better of us."

James snorted. "A little late for that, isn't it?"

All eyes turned toward him, and I saw the flicker of something cold and calculating in his gaze. I had noticed it at the rehearsal dinner, and now it was even more apparent. What was he hiding?

"James," Savannah said quietly, her voice barely above a whisper. "Please don't."

Please don't what? I wondered what Savannah meant by that. I glanced between her and James. Stephen scrutinized them too.

Allen had arrived back at the inn and had slipped into the dining room unnoticed while I'd been busy in the kitchen. Now he stood by the door, his arms crossed, watching everyone with the intensity of a hawk surveying its prey. He was testing them—testing all of us, I realized.

But before James could respond to Savannah, Allen cleared his throat. "I think it's time we address the issue at hand." His voice cut through the room, commanding everyone's attention. "I found an antique revolver in the orchard earlier today. It's currently being tested for fingerprints and ballistics. If it's the murder weapon, we'll know soon. I need to know who was familiar with the gun collection and case inside the study."

A sharp intake of breath filled the room. Hugh shifted uncomfortably in his seat, while Martha's hand shot to her mouth, her eyes widening in shock.

Savannah looked at Allen, her voice trembling. "You think someone ... here ... used that gun?"

Allen's gaze didn't waver. "I'm not ruling anyone out, Miss Collier."

The silence that followed was deafening. I could feel the mistrust pulsing between them—between all of us. Someone in this room knew more than they were letting on.

Beatrice leaned forward, her voice soft but firm. "Detective, do you really think any of us could be responsible for this? We're family. We've known each other for years."

"Not everyone is family and family doesn't mean innocence," Allen replied, his eyes never leaving hers.

I glanced at Tom, who had been standing by the kitchen door, his face expressionless as he watched the scene unfold. Even he looked tense, his usual calm demeanor shaken. As our eyes met, I wondered if he had his own suspicions—he always noticed things others didn't.

"I can't stay here," Martha suddenly announced, standing up so abruptly that her chair scraped loudly against the floor. "This ... this is too much." She glared at Hugh, then turned to Savannah. "We're leaving tomorrow. I won't spend another night under this roof."

"Martha don't be ridiculous," Beatrice snapped. "What about Stephen and Savannah's wedding? Surely ..."

"I don't care!" Martha interrupted in a shrill voice, on the verge of breaking. "My husband is dead, and all of you—" Her eyes darted to James, then Susan, then Hugh. "—you're all just sitting here, plotting to steal his money."

"Mama!" Savannah cried, reaching for her arm.

But it was too late. The dam had broken. Martha stormed out of the room. Savannah followed close behind. The rest of us sat frozen, the shock settling over the table like a heavy fog.

I looked at Allen, who stood silently by the door, his expression unreadable. He gave me a small, tight nod, and I knew what he was thinking.

This wasn't over. Far from it.

Chapter Four

Midnight Sleuth

The house seemed eerily quiet. Lily and Lionel had left hours ago; their help wasn't needed without the wedding reception going forward. Tom had gone home to rest after he and Sally had cleaned up the dinner dishes. He wouldn't be back until early morning to start his regular daily routine.

First thing in the morning, I normally collected the eggs from the hen house, fed the chickens and other animals, while Tom prepared breakfast for the inn guests. Sally Rawlins was my only staff that lived in with me. She was a blessing. I had hired Sally last fall as a housekeeper. She was a recent widow, in her early fifties, with salt and pepper pixie-cut hair and a pleasantly round shape. Her husband's death left her without life insurance or other means to support herself, forcing her to sell her small home. Her only son lived in Oregon, and her one spinster sister resided in Raleigh. Sally, determined to remain independent and not be a burden on her family, readily accepted my offer as housekeeper for the inn. She shared the third floor with me. We each had our own bedroom but shared the connecting Jack and Jill bathroom. With Sally I didn't have to worry about her snooping into my possessions like I did when my cousin Bobbie Jo had occupied that bedroom. Sally was quiet, a good worker, and moved about the inn performing her duties as invisible as a ghost. Maybe more so, considering how Grannie's ghost could intrude at times.

Rocking gently on the porch glider, my finger twirled a lock of hair as my mind drifted on the cool evening breeze. It didn't surprise me when I glanced up to find Allen joining me.

"Want some company?" he asked.

"Love some. Are you comfortable enough in the meadow flower room? Sorry to put you in such a frilly room, but it's the only vacant room I had."

Allen laughed. "I think I'll survive the pink walls and dainty flowers as long as the guys from the precinct don't see me sleeping in that canopy bed."

My mind conjured up an image of his muscular body reclining on soft cotton sheets across that bed. A hot blush colored my face and I prayed he didn't guess where my imagination had taken me. I turned away and pretended to search for Luke while the night air cooled my face. Luckily for me, Luke greeted us with a bark as he climbed the porch steps then sprawled at our feet. Allen reached down and scratched behind his ears. Luke wagged his tail and tilted his big head, eager for Allen's touch. The shepherd had found a friend in the Yankee.

"Will you allow everyone to leave tomorrow?" I asked.

"As soon as I get the fingerprint reports back. Yes. We've got everyone's statements. I dusted your gun cabinet for prints too. Sorry. I know it makes a mess but I'm sure your housekeeper can wipe off the black powder. I'm eager to see who's accessed that glass case and if we have a matching print from the cabinet to the gun."

"Guess that will identify your killer then. Is that right? Do you have any ideas? Who do you suspect?" I asked.

"I suspect them all. Any one of them had opportunity and possible motive."

"Surely, not everyone. Savannah and Stephen were in the house with us when we heard the gun shot. They couldn't have done it." I searched my memory of that moment in time when we dashed out of the house and ran to the barn. Lily and Lionel were there, plus Allen and me. Stephen and Savannah entered the barn behind us. Who did that leave absent?

"I'd rather wait on the forensic findings and evidence. I don't put much store in hunches."

"Sometimes, hunches are all you have," I murmured.

"You've had a long day. Maybe it's best if we turn in," Allen said as he rose from the glider and headed inside.

"C'mon Luke. Let's lock up. Time for bed."

I entered the house and went about my usual routine, locking the front door, turning on a small lamp in the foyer, and checked the lock on the back door. Luke sought his food bowl and water in the kitchen then trotted behind me. The house was secure as I trudged up the stairs to the third floor and my bedroom haven.

Slipping into the bathroom, I silently made my night time ablutions. I could hear Sally's deep breathing and light snoring coming from the other side of the door. Careful not to wake her, I finished and crept back into my own room. Luke had stretched out across the bottom of my mattress, enjoying the comfortable landing spot.

The night sky appeared darker than usual with the moon gliding in and out of dense clouds. There was a scent of moisture in the air. Likely rain would start soon. I cracked my bedroom windows open to allow the night air to cool the room. Staring into the black night, I glimpsed Prissy in the faint moonlight on her nightly prowl hunting for the unwary mouse. In the distance, tree frogs croaked their nocturnal song. Dropping the sheer curtains back into place, I turned away from the window but stopped when a glimmer of light caught my eye. Was I imagining it? I stared into the inky night. Yes! There it was again. A quick flash of light coming from the barn. Stepping into a pair of slippers, I hurried out of my room. Luke jumped off the bed excitedly and followed as I dashed down the stairs to the second floor.

Tapping lightly on door number four, the meadow flower room, I hoped Allen hadn't fallen asleep yet. He pulled the door open and stared at me. I wished I had taken the time to pull on my robe as his eyes raked my body, taking in my flimsy nightgown attire and slippers. I felt a hot blush color my cheeks.

"What's wrong?" he asked. His hair appeared rumpled. He wore just a white t-shirt over a pair of soft jeans with bare feet.

"I saw a light shining outside. Come quick. I think someone's in the barn with a flashlight."

He slipped shoes on and closed the door behind him as we hurried down the stairs and into the kitchen. The back door stood unlatched.

"I locked that door before I went upstairs; I know I did." Luke shot out the door ahead of us into the yard.

Allen nodded then pressed his finger against his lips to indicate silence. We crept toward the barn entrance. Allen motioned me to allow him to lead and I gratefully hung back. His right hand held a weapon—his nine millimeter automatic. I realized I hadn't noticed it before. Just the sight of the detective's gun made me gulp and understand we were dealing with a potential murderer.

Suddenly, lightning cracked ... a brilliant streak flashed across the black sky. I smelled the ozone in the air. Heavy drops of rain pelted the metal barn roof like scattered marbles before the sky opened and a deluge of water let loose. We quickly took refuge under the roof over-hang, but I could feel my back getting wet before we eased the barn door open wide enough to slide inside. Standing in the shadows, we strained to listen. I shivered from both my wet nightgown and my sudden fear.

My eyes had adjusted to the dark, yet I could only make out shapes of the tables and chairs positioned within the cavernous space. Plenty of hiding places. I anxiously waited by the door, holding tight to Luke's collar while he growled softly. Allen moved soundlessly down one side of the room. He crept past the bandstand; I could just make out his form in the blackness as he began to search the other perimeter.

Why had someone returned to the barn and the scene of the crime? What was there to gain? Could he or she be searching for something? I doubted the forensic team had missed anything in their thorough sweep of the area. So, what could possibly be left?

All of a sudden, an indignant feline shriek rent the air as Allen stepped on Prissy. The cat leaped in the air and I heard Allen stumble and curse. Simultaneously, I screamed as a man rushed past me, knocking me to the ground, then bolted out the barn door. Luke barked and charged into the night. Allen rushed toward me and the open portal.

"Are you all right?" He questioned as he paused before pursuing the suspect into the night.

"Yes. Go. Be careful." I took a deep breath to calm my shaky nerves as Prissy swaggered over and rubbed her back against my legs. Picking her up, I petted her glossy coat and cuddled her warm body to me. She answered me with a deep purring sound.

"What are you doing in here, missy? You aren't supposed to sleep in the barn any more. Didn't I make you a nice cozy spot in the garden shed? Hmm? How did you get in here again?" As I questioned the cat, I suddenly realized she had to have followed our intruder. The cat couldn't have opened the heavy barn door nor were there any other entrances for her to crawl through.

The summer cloud burst had ended. Steam rose from the wet ground and the increased humidity produced a cloying sauna.

Outside, Luke barked and trotted around the perimeter of the yard, stopping to sniff here and there, then returned to Allen's side. I waited with Prissy by the barn entrance.

"Whoever it was, he's gone, slipped away. That darn cat ..."

"Prissy was outside previously. I saw her hunting. She must have followed whoever opened the barn door. She sleeps in the garden shed with her kittens. See?" I pointed to the garden shed; its door hung ajar. "This door shouldn't be open either."

I pulled the door open wider and yanked the string for the overhead light. Four tiny kittens mewed, disturbed by the bright light. They cuddled together into a ball of fur on the thick pet bed in the back of the shed. Rakes, hoes, and shovels hung neatly on hooks along the shed's walls. Buckets, hand trowels, and gardening gloves rested on a long shelf.

"One of the shovels is missing. There was a long handled shovel hanging right there," I pointed to an empty hook.

"You sure? Could Tom have forgotten to put it away?"

"No, Tom is very particular about his tools. I'm certain a shovel is missing. I don't understand. First an antique pistol is buried and now someone is searching the grounds. What's going on?"

"I don't know, but I'm going to get to the bottom of it," Allen said as we slowly made our way back to the house after locking up the barn and closing the shed. Prissy crawled through the pet entry hinged on the bottom of the shed door to join her waiting kittens.

As we entered the kitchen, I spotted muddy footprints on the tiled floor. Good gracious! He was in the house. Whoever our suspect was, he had foolishly left a trail. Following the tracks, we left the kitchen, creeped into the hall, and moved toward the staircase, but the footprints had disappeared. Allen and I looked at each other; a frown wrinkled Allen's brow. Either our culprit had removed his shoes or he disappeared into thin air.

Chapter Five

Unfinished Deal

I stood by the large window in the Magnolia Blossom Inn's living room, staring out at the empty apple orchard. Even the aroma of Tom's freshly baked bread couldn't lighten my mood. The setting sun cast long shadows across the rows of apple trees, but all I could see was that revolver we had found earlier, buried near the orchard's edge. One of Granddaddy Charles' prize possessions had been used to kill Stanton Collier. I still couldn't come to grips with that. Now the question was— who would do such a thing?

The house seemed strangely quiet now that Savannah and her mother had vacated, along with the Beauregard family earlier this morning. Even Susan Harper had made her excuses to exit the inn. Sally and I had spent the day busily stripping sheets and cleaning bathrooms within the empty suites. I had hoped to uncover a pair of muddy shoes or at least some evidence of that effect while turning the rooms, but no luck. I'd even purposefully studied everyone's feet when they checked out too, but all appeared clean and normal. Another dead end.

Allen sat at the dining room table, drumming his fingers impatiently on the wood. He'd been waiting for the forensic team to report back on the gun fingerprints and ballistics. I knew him well enough by now to see the frustration boiling just beneath the surface. He wanted answers, and so did I.

"I found something," he said, spreading out creased papers in front of him as I entered the room. He wore a grim expression. "In Collier's room. I sneaked in while his widow finished her breakfast. Papers—contracts. Looks like he was involved in some sort of deal with James Warner."

My stomach knotted. "What kind of deal?"

"Treasure hunting," Allen replied, handing me a folded sheet of paper. "Apparently, Stanton Collier was planning to invest a sizable amount of money into a hunt for Civil War treasure rumored to be buried on your land. But something went wrong. There's a note at the bottom where Collier called it off."

"That's ridiculous. I've never heard any rumor about treasure. I majored in history at UV. If Civil War treasure was buried in this part of the country, don't you think I'd have learned about it in my studies? My family has lived here since 1830; we've struggled to keep this property over decades of tough times. If there was truly a hidden fortune, my family would have cashed in on it years ago."

I scanned the document, noting Stanton's scrawled signature at the bottom and the hasty, angry note canceling the deal. "So, James was after more than just being best man in the wedding. He was hoping to strike it rich by being at Magnolia Blossom."

Allen nodded. "Looks that way. And now Collier's dead, and the deal's off permanently."

"What are you going to do about it?"

"Confront Warner with the facts and see what he says."

As if our thoughts had conjured up the man, I turned to see James Warner stroll in, wearing that casual smirk of his. I'd love to wipe it off his face. He acted like this was just another day in his con artist world, not the aftermath of a murder that had shattered a family.

"Is this a private party? So, Maddie," James said, leaning casually against the doorframe, "I guess the inn's staying pretty empty now, what with the wedding party all trickling out."

"Except for you," I replied. Ignoring his question, I kept my voice steady. "You seem pretty comfortable sticking around after everything that's happened."

He shrugged. "Well, the room's paid for until Monday, so why not? Besides, I've got unfinished business."

That was exactly what Allen and I wanted to learn.

Before I could respond, Grannie's voice whispered in my ear, soft and fleeting. *"Don't let him dig too deep, Maddie. It'll bring ruin…"*

I paused and tried to appear nonchalant. Grannie's warnings were always vague. I wished she could just spell it out for me—what ruin? Who was she talking about? Why did ghosts have to be so cryptic?

Allen's chair scraped back as he stood, crossing the room with the intent of a man on a mission. His eyes fixed on James. "You and I need to talk. About that treasure hunt you and Stanton had planned."

James's smile faltered, just for a second. "Treasure hunt? I don't know what you're talking about."

Allen stepped closer, his jaw tightening. "Let's not play games. I've already read the contract we found in Stanton's room. You were in this together, searching for some fabled Civil War plunder. But I'm guessing things didn't go as smoothly as you hoped."

I watched as James's bravado slipped a notch. His fingers fidgeted with a college ring on his finger, twisting and turning it, a telltale sign of guilt if I'd ever seen one.

"Fine," he muttered, crossing his arms. "Stanton and I had an agreement. He'd bankroll the search, and I'd get a share if we found anything. But the man got greedy. He wanted more than just his share—he demanded it all. Said he'd cut me out. That's why I was here."

Allen's gaze sharpened. "Here for what? Revenge?"

James chuckled darkly. "Revenge? No, Detective. I was here to renegotiate. I wasn't stupid enough to kill him. I needed him alive if I wanted a shot at that treasure. Seemed the perfect opportunity, kill two birds with one stone, so to speak. Offer my services as best man to an old friend and speak to Collier about our agreement, maybe even get to do a little treasure hunting."

"Where were you last night, around midnight?" asked Allen, his eyes studying every tick in James' face.

"Asleep in my room. Why?"

"Can you prove it?" Allen demanded.

"Of course I can't prove it. I was sleeping and so was Stephen. If he wasn't, I wouldn't know it and neither would he if I had gotten up. You'll just have to take my word for it that I didn't leave my room until breakfast." Warner dragged a hand through his hair then spun on his heel to leave. "I guess no more suppers are being offered, so I'm gonna go into town to find something to eat. I assume I'm not under arrest, detective?"

"You're free to go. For now. I know where to find you."

We watched him saunter out of the house and climb into his car.

Tom entered the room, wiping his hands on a towel; he glanced between me and the detective.

His forehead grooved in a deep frown, a mask of concern on his face, he said, "We've got a problem. Sally is missing."

"What do you mean, missing?" I asked, my heart rate spiking.

"I can't find her anywhere. She's gone," Tom said.

I rushed up the stairs then knocked softly on the bedroom door next to my own, then again, louder. No answer.

"Sally?" I called, worry prickling at the back of my neck. I twisted the doorknob and pushed the door open.

The room was empty.

Her bed was neatly made, her uniform laid across the chair, as if she had planned to change soon. But there was no sign of Sally. A folded piece of paper lay on her pillow, with my name scrawled across it. I unfolded the note with trembling hands:

"Maddie, I'm sorry. They made me help. I'm scared." Sally

My heart dropped. What had she done and who was *they*? Why had she run? Was she really that scared, or was she too involved?

I slowly returned to Tom and Allen waiting outside on the porch. Both men gripped cups of hot coffee. Tom held out a cup to me as I sank onto the glider.

"She's gone," I blurted out, holding up the note. "Sally's run away."

Allen's eyes narrowed as he read the note. "Judas Priest! This case just gets more complicated."

Chapter Six

Historic Secrets

Allen's cell phone rang. He frowned as he read the number. "I've got to take this," he said.

I nodded as he paced the length of the porch, the phone pressed to his ear. He turned and stopped by my chair.

"I've got to get back to the station. Forensics finished the fingerprint report plus ballistic findings. With Warner still staying here, I don't like the idea of leaving you alone with him."

"Tom is here for awhile. I'll call Lily and Lionel and ask them to come out. I'd be a fool not to admit that James Warner makes me feel nervous. I don't trust him. He makes my skin crawl. I know you've got your work to do and can't babysit me but I'll be okay."

"Are you sure?"

"Of course. I'd leave too but I don't want to allow Warner free run of my property in my absence. I'd probably come back to half the land dug up with his treasure hunting!"

"I'm here with you, baby girl. That scalawag won't hurt you with me around," Grannie chortled. Her ghostly image lingered near the front entry.

"Call your friends now. I won't go until I'm reassured they'll be here with you," Allen said. He squeezed my hand and tried to inject a level of calm into me I wasn't feeling.

I nodded as I opened my cell phone and pressed Lionel's number. A smile curled my lips as my dear friend answered on the second ring.

"Hey Maddie girl, what's up?" Lionel greeted me.

"Are you busy? Can you come out? Everyone is gone except James Warner and I'd rather not be alone with him. Detective Crawford is returning to Charlottesville to study the forensic reports. And if all that isn't reason enough, I could use your help with some internet research. So what do you say? Can you drive out?"

"Of course I can. You know I'd drop everything for you. I'll be there in twenty minutes with my laptop in hand."

"Thanks, you're the best. And Lionel, better pack a toothbrush and plan on staying over."

"Ooh, slumber party! Is Lily coming? Sounds like fun."

"I'm phoning her next. Maybe we'll get lucky and she hasn't been called back to the hospital," I said.

I ended the call and looked at Allen.

"Okay," he said. "If Lionel is on the way, then I'll go ahead and leave. You should be all right. You can always lock yourself inside the house. Warner can't get in without a key, if worse comes to worse."

"Gee, you make me feel so safe," I jested. "Go on. I know you're chomping at the bit to read that forensic report. Promise me you'll phone and let me know the results, or at least as much as you can. The suspense will be killing me."

"I'll try and do that." Allen reached down and rubbed the shepherd's big head. "You take care of her, Luke."

Luke shook his head and gave a short bark in agreement.

Thirty minutes later, it felt good to laugh and relax with my friends as we sat around the farmhouse kitchen table. Lionel had stopped along his drive and brought a bucket of fried chicken. We munched on the yummy chicken and ate bowls of salad greens plus heaping spoonfuls of creamy baked macaroni and cheese that Tom had prepared for us along with his tasty homemade bread. It was a delicious and simple feast. I peered at Lily as she daintily held a chicken drumstick, her pinky finger curled under. No matter what Lily was engaged in, from performing surgery to eating fried chicken, her mannerisms remained graceful and delicate, like the porcelain doll she resembled. Pouring another glass of sweet tea for Lionel, I smiled at my dear friends who had rallied to my needs. I appreciated the sacrifice of their precious time, more than they would ever know. Now it was time to get to work.

"We need to prove or disprove the theory of Confederate treasure being hidden in this part of Albemarle County. I never heard any tales of treasure, especially not on our farm, but the chance of a buried fortune has caused a man to be murdered. If I don't stop this false rumor, I'm afraid more crime will happen."

"Don't worry, Maddie. Between your knowledge of American history and my expert research skills, we'll dig up this so-called plunder. Pardon my pun," Lionel said with a laugh as he wiped his hands and opened his laptop.

I laughed at his quip. "All right. Let's see what you can dig up then."

We divided our search into three categories: the history of Charlottesville, specific Civil War events in Albemarle County, and biographical history of famous Confederates of the region. We each concentrated on a topic and got busy with our laptops. Lionel delved into the biographies, I researched battles, and Lily read through the county history. Our fingers flew across keyboards, printing out anything relative, and drilling down into layers of ancestry that crisscrossed prominent families of the South.

"This feels like we're back in university," Lily commented as she jotted notes on a yellow legal pad.

After two hours, I stood and stretched my arms. I rolled my head and cramped neck from side to side to work out the kinks.

"Let's take a break and share what we've got so far. Y'all care for something to drink?" I asked.

"Would you have a beer on hand?" asked Lionel as he peeked inside the refrigerator. "Ah, yeah, a Corona. Thanks, Tom. Want one?" he asked as he held up the bottle.

"No, you have one. Lily and I can finish off that bottle of zinfandel on the fridge door."

We settled back with our drinks then passed around the printouts to read each other's findings. Lily was delighted in learning Charlottesville had contained a large military hospital during the war run by a Dr. J.L. Cabell. She shared his interesting medical notes on patient care. But unless you counted bandages, artificial limbs, and bloody body parts— there was no hidden fortune associated in the hospital. The old building had been torn down years ago.

Reading aloud, I shared my information on a Union raid that involved Charlottesville and General George Custer. Fascinating stuff that a historian like me ate up. "The cavalry raided the city in February of 1864 in what later became known as the Kilpatrick-Dahlgren Raid. It was a maneuver meant to distract from the true objective of freeing Union prisoners held in Richmond. During the skirmish, Confederate General J.E.B. Stuart won acclaim as the hero of the battle of Rio Hill with his Stuart Horse Artillery unit. I didn't find any mention of a cache of money left behind in the raid."

"I always did think ole Jeb was a dashing dude," Lionel remarked as he scanned the battle information. "Hey, did you know the Confederacy minted both gold and silver coins in three places: New Orleans; Dahlonega, Georgia, and as nearby as Charlotte, North Carolina? It's not too farfetched to think some of those coins could have made their way into Virginia. Pretty cool, huh?"

"Really? Hmm, I didn't know there was a mint in Charlotte. That's interesting. I imagine Stuart's troopers and that hospital staff Lily read about would all require a payroll. Hey, what if they were paid in coin instead of paper money? Of course, that still doesn't prove that any of that money made its way to my family's farm."

"What does Grannie say?" asked Lily in a voice just above a whisper. She quickly glanced over her shoulder as if merely speaking her name would make Grannie materialize.

As if Lily's inquiry worked, a sensation of cold air announced Grannie's arrival.

"Goodness, y'all been busy. Hunting in books and historical stories won't solve your mystery. You need to direct your search closer to home," Grannie said then disappeared in a poof.

"What did she mean, closer to home?" Lily asked.

"I'm uncertain, but we had an intruder in the barn last night. Allen and I followed him when we spotted a flash of light, but we lost him. Let's go back and inspect the barn and yard again. Maybe Grannie meant for us to look closer to home in the barn, like where Stanton died," I said.

"Where's Sally? How's she taking all this crime drama swirling around? I know Tom goes home after five, but usually I see Sally bustling about," Lionel said as he carried his empty place to the sink and ran water over it.

I pulled the note paper out of my pocket and silently handed it to Lionel. Lily peered over his shoulder and gasped at the message.

"She left? Was she involved in the murder? Oh my goodness!" Lily's hand flew to her mouth and rested there. She raised her almond eyes to me in disbelief.

"Honestly, I don't know what to think. I found the note on her bed; her room was empty and she had left."

"Wow! I never would have suspected Sally. Does she have any connection with the Collier family? Her note says she was forced. Who forced her and what did she do?" asked Lionel.

"I have no idea. I'm trying to keep an open mind. I don't want to think she's capable of murder."

"Do the police suspect her of murder?" asked Lily.

"No ... I don't think so. That is ... Allen didn't say so. I wish he'd call with the results of that fingerprint test."

"Tell me more about this light you saw and the intruder," Lionel said, his voice taking on a grave tone.

"Um, I had just gone up to bed when I looked out my bedroom window and noticed a light shining in the barn, like a flashlight. Allen was staying over so I went to his room and told him then we both hurried out to the barn. By the time we got there, we couldn't find anyone but then I got knocked down when the culprit rushed out of the dark. Allen tried following him but we lost his tracks."

"That hunky detective stayed over? How deliciously cozy!" Lionel jested, the one fact he had chosen to concentrate on.

"Never mind that Lionel," Lily said as she smacked him in the arm, then turned to me. "What do you think he was looking for in the barn?" Lily asked.

"I don't know. It's silly, really. That barn isn't even original to the property. We have a concrete floor, not dirt. It's not likely someone buried a treasure chest under the floor. Remember that box of old pictures that I found last year? There were photos of the house and barn from back in the 1950s. Grannie told me lightning hit the barn in 1953 and it burnt to the ground. This barn dates back to then, not Civil War years. Any hidden treasure from the 1860s would certainly have been found after the fire and during the reconstruction of the new barn a hundred years later."

"That makes sense," Lionel followed the logical thought process.

"But unless you were familiar with the farm and your family, no one would know the history of the building," Lily surmised.

"Good point. Somebody probably thinks the barn could still hold a hidden prize," Lionel said.

"Exactly. So, before it gets any darker, do you want to take a stroll out there and have a look around? I'd really like your opinion." I said. I locked the front door of the house while we were occupied in the barn, erring on caution with so much going on.

"Sure. Let's do it. It'll be an adventure," Lionel agreed, jumping up, and the three of us trooped out of the house and across the yard. Luke ran and jumped in glee, ready to play, as he joined us.

I pulled open the large barn door. My hand touched the bank of light switches on the wall and high canned lights in the ceiling sparked to life, illuminating the spacious room. Banquet tables and round guest tables still wore their rose pink tablecloths. The flowers in bud vases hung in sad wilted postures. I couldn't help the tears that came to my eyes as I surveyed the tragic scene.

By silent agreement, we gave a wide berth to the spot where Stanton Collier's body had lain. We separated and strolled around the empty building, poking our heads here and there into storage bins, around sound systems, and looked under the raised band platform. Luke sniffed and pawed at the floor then shook his head and followed us throughout the barn. As we approached the rear corner of the barn where the false door had been, I pointed to the new siding. Luke barked and scratched at the wood panel.

"What's got him riled up?" Lionel asked as he examined the siding.

"Maybe he's remembering the trouble from last year. Tom and I agreed it was best to nail shut that hinged panel that Bobbie Jo had used to escape the barn last year. I wouldn't want anyone using that to sneak in or out of my party room."

"Is that why the wood looks different in this corner of the barn? Wouldn't it appear newer and not older?" asked Lily.

She ran her hand along the wide wood panels, tracing the grain patterns. It did look older. I never noticed that before.

"The old barn didn't burn completely down. Charlie's father built the new barn around it and connected to the original walls," Grannie said as she hovered overhead. *"See where I carved my initials into that panel?"*

Grannie's historical tidbit surprised us all as we stared at the engraved wood.

Chapter Seven

Secret Passage

We headed outside to circle the barn. The early evening sun had dipped below the horizon, casting everything in a deep orange glow. The orchard beyond swayed gently in the evening breeze, but there was an eerie quiet in the air. Luke seemed uneasy, sticking close to my side as we approached the weathered barn siding in the rear. A long-handled shovel lay in the brush between the hen house and vegetable garden. Was that Tom's missing shovel? Luke growled and pawed at the ground, digging in the earth near the corner of the building. Oh no, please don't let him uncover another buried revolver ... or worse.

Wind picked up and rustled through the apple trees. The shadows of dusk created an ominous atmosphere that made me tremble. What was that old saying? Like someone walked over my grave? I shivered again.

As the dog dug, a metal hinge came into sight under the shallow dirt. Luke barked, proud of his efforts. Lionel and I both crouched, dropped onto our knees, and cleared the shallow soil away from what appeared to be a hinged trapdoor set into the ground.

"Maybe it's a root cellar or it could be a storm cellar. I read where folks dug root cellars to store fruits and vegetables during the winter back before refrigeration was invented," Lily commented.

"You're right, that's probably all this is … a root cellar. Makes sense that there would be one near the barn and orchards," I said, trying to reason with my nerves and squash a sense of pending doom.

Lionel cleared off the remaining dirt and ran his fingers around the edges of the wood door. It wasn't clogged with hardened earth, making me wonder when it had been last opened. With a strong yank, Lionel lifted the door. We stared into a pitch black hole. A narrow ladder leaning against the cellar wall led downward.

Luke let out a low growl, his ears pinned back.

"We need more flashlights," Lionel said.

"You aren't thinking of going down there, are you?" Lily asked in a voice filled with tension. She put her hand on Lionel's arm to halt him.

"I'm coming too. This is my property. I need to see what's down there. Wait. Don't do anything until I grab some more lights. I'll be right back."

I ran the short distance to the house and dashed into the kitchen. Yanking open the broom closet, I grabbed two battery-powered lanterns from the shelf. We always kept extra light sources on hand in case of storm power outages. They'd be perfect for exploring the cellar.

The night air was thick with the scent of damp earth and ripe fruit as Lionel and I stood over the open root cellar door behind the barn. My heart pounded in my chest as we stared into the yawning darkness below. The need for caution warred with my impulsive desire to see what was down there.

"You ready for this?" Lionel asked, his voice wavering only slightly, but the tension in his body betrayed the calm facade.

"Don't you think we should call the police? Let them investigate," Lily said, worry etching her face.

Luke barked, a low growl rumbled in the back of his throat. He pawed at the edge of the opening and top of the ladder.

"No boy, you can't go down there," I said as I patted his back. He lowered into a sitting position, alert but in a relaxed stance.

I handed a lantern to Lionel then turned mine on. The LED bulbs glowed brightly. Holding the light above the ladder, I tried to peer into the depth.

"I'll go first," Lionel volunteered.

"Okay. Be careful. I'll be right behind you."

"Maybe I better stay up here in case something goes wrong and you need help," Lily suggested.

"Scaredy cat. Okay. You call for rescue if we don't come back," I teased.

"That's not funny, Maddie. You don't know what you'll find down there. Be careful. If it doesn't smell right, get out of there. You don't know what kind of toxic substances might be buried in there either." Lily, always the cautious physician, gave us one last warning as Lionel turned and placed a foot on the ladder rungs and started backwards into the chasm.

As we descended into the cellar, the wooden ladder creaked under our weight. Twice the ladder shifted against the wall and we paused our descent, praying the structure wouldn't fall and take us with it. The temperature dropped as we went deeper, the air stale and cold.

My feet finally hit the bottom. I peered up at least fifteen feet above my head to see Lily and Luke, outlined in the evening sky, bending over the entrance. The cellar smelled like musty, stinky gym shoes. I hated that smell; it was like being back in a school's locker room. The earthen walls were damp to the touch. Narrow wooden planks lined the floor. I could see small puddles of water under the planks that had seeped up from the ground after the last rain. A tunnel stretched into a black void to our left. Lionel and I stood at the base of the ladder and held our lanterns above our heads to study the space.

"Well ... guess we go that way," Lionel said softly as he pointed his light toward the tunnel.

"Does this look like a normal root cellar? I thought there'd be shelving or something, you know, to hold mason jars." I gulped as I considered the void ahead. My courage was waning.

We slowly moved forward. I swallowed a shriek and clutched Lionel's arm as a mouse ran across my foot and scurried into the blackness. The tunnel took a bend then widened. We followed it, holding our breaths. The dark cavern absorbed my meager light.

I swept my light across the immediate open space, revealing rows of shelves filled with dusty jars and rusted tools—remnants of another era. Now that was what I had expected a root cellar to look like. I turned full circle. However, it wasn't old jars that caught my eye. At the far end of the cellar, in the dim glow of my lantern ... I saw her.

"Sally!" I gasped, rushing forward, Lionel right behind me.

She was bound to a wooden chair, her head slumped forward, unconscious. A black cloth covered her eyes; a trickle of blood had dripped down her head and dried on her cheek. Thick ropes circled her wrists and ankles, and a rag had been stuffed into her mouth, secured with a strip of cloth around her head.

"Oh my God," Lionel whispered, horror spreading across his face. "What the hell ... ?"

I dropped to my knees beside her, checking her pulse. It was faint, but she was alive. Relief surged through me, but anger quickly replaced it. Whoever had done this to her wasn't just after treasure—they were playing a dangerous game.

"Help me get her untied," I said, my voice shaking as I worked at the knots binding her wrists. I pulled the blindfold off her face and removed the gag.

Lionel crouched down and started on her ankles. "Who could've done this? And why?"

I didn't have an answer, and even if I did, I couldn't say it out loud. Not with the knots of fear twisting tighter in my chest. But I couldn't ignore the gnawing suspicion that whoever had tied Sally up knew exactly how to use this cellar to their advantage.

Just as we freed her, Sally's eyelids fluttered open, her eyes wild with confusion and fear. She coughed, her dry mouth struggled to form words.

"Who ... who's there?" she rasped.

"It's me, Maddie," I said gently, laying a hand on her shoulder. "You're safe now."

Tears welled up in her eyes as she shook her head weakly.

"No ... no, they're coming back." She slipped back into unconsciousness.

"Who?" Lionel demanded, his tone sharper than usual as his fear for Sally seeped into his words. "Who's coming back?"

"We need to get out of here."

Lionel swore under his breath. "I'll carry her. Whatever or whoever is down here, we're not sticking around to find out."

I nodded, feeling the weight of my foolish decision to explore pressing down on me. Lily was right ... I needed to call the police. I helped Lionel lift Sally, who hung limply in his arms.

That's when I noticed it—a narrow passage behind us in the shadows, almost hidden behind a row of shelves. The tunnel opening was just wide enough for a person to squeeze through. I shone the flashlight down its length. It seemed to stretch on forever into a black void; old crumbling stone lined the walls. My light faded into a small circle.

"Looks like it could lead under the house," Lionel muttered, seeing where my attention focused and shifting Sally's weight in his arms.

"Good gracious, a secret entrance into our basement? I'll never sleep soundly in that house again," I said, shuddering.

"We'll come back for answers later," Lionel said.

"Let's get Sally out of here," I said, my voice low but firm.

Lionel didn't argue, and we turned back toward the ladder, moving quickly. But as we reached the base of the ladder, I saw a shadowy figure standing above in the entrance. My heart caught in my throat then I breathed a sigh of relief. I'd forgotten Lily, her face pale in the beam of my flashlight.

"Maddie, I—I called Allen," she stammered, her voice barely above a whisper. "I saw something moving in the yard. I got scared and—"

Before she could finish, I heard an engine roaring in the distance, followed by the crunch of tires on gravel. A moment later, Allen's silhouette appeared next to Lily behind the barn, gun drawn.

"Everyone okay?" he called out, his voice tight as he peered into the hole. "What were you thinking of, running off on your own to explore a dangerous cavern? I thought you had better common sense than that!" He practically growled the last words.

I ignored his reprimand and pointed out the obvious.

"We found her," I called up, nodding toward Sally. "She's alive, but barely. Stop yelling at me and help us get her up the ladder. Lionel will lift her in a fireman carry but you need to catch her at the top."

Allen's eyes darkened as he holstered his gun. He laid down on the ground and reached into the dark cellar, as Lionel slowly climbed the ladder. He grabbed Sally under her arms and lifted her weight from Lionel's shoulders as he pulled her to the surface.

Lily knelt beside Sally, checking her over with the practiced hand of a professional. "We need to get her to a hospital, fast."

"Do you think whoever did this is still here?" Lionel asked, his voice full of suspicion.

Allen glanced at the deep cellar then shook his head. "I doubt it. Not anymore. Let's get her out of here first, and then we'll come back. I want a thorough search of this entire property by my team. This place holds more secrets than Merlin's closet."

As we made our way back toward the house, the tension between us was palpable. I couldn't shake the feeling that we were being watched. The shadows themselves were hiding more than just old secrets. Whoever had tied Sally up had done it to send a message—they played for keeps and would stop at nothing.

Chapter Eight

Cobwebs and Footprints

The next morning, the police swarmed the Magnolia Blossom Inn, the flashing lights of their cruisers reflected off the dew-slicked lawn. I stood at the back porch, watching Allen and his team comb through the property again, concentrating behind the barn. Lionel paced beside me, restless energy coursing through him. We had recounted every little detail of what we had found in the tunnel to Allen. I could barely think straight. The events of the last few hours swirled in my head like a southern storm.

"So you're telling me there's an entire underground maze beneath the property?" Allen asked, arms crossed, a skeptical look on his face.

"Seems like it," I said, folding my arms across my chest.

Lionel nodded, too wound up to even be sarcastic. "Yeah, man. We're talking old stone walls, tunnels that lead from the root cellar probably back to the basement of the house. It's like something out of a horror movie."

I could tell Allen wasn't fully buying it yet, but he had bigger things to worry about—like James Warner, who was still sitting pretty inside the inn, pretending like he hadn't just tried to con two families with a bogus Civil War treasure story.

Allen glanced at me, a half-smile tugging at the corner of his mouth. "Let me guess—you didn't mention anything about Confederate coins to the wedding guests when you were selling the place as a venue."

"Of course not," I said, wrapping a strand of hair around my finger. "I told you that's a myth. I was just hoping for a nice wedding ... you know, flowers, music, no murder, no buried treasure. But here we are."

He chuckled, shaking his head. "Mm-hmm, welcome to small-town Virginia. I'll take Philadelphia's hard core crime any day."

Lionel was still pacing, his hands flailing. "But the thing is, if it's true, Maddie's granddad must've known about it. Confederate gold has been a local legend for years, but no one really believed it. Now people are tearing up barns and kidnapping housekeepers for it."

I sighed, running a hand through my hair. "Granddaddy Charles never told me anything about a treasure, buried or otherwise. Grannie ... well, she kept a lot of things to herself. This whole Confederate cache of gold is just a story, something told on cold winter nights to pass the time. It's ridiculous. I've stopped answering my phone because either reporters or Clarkstown gossips want to hear all about the treasure."

"I don't want either of you running off half-cocked and exploring that underground cellar on your own. Promise me?" Allen demanded as he looked pointedly at Lionel then back to me.

Allen glanced over at the house, where James Warner was sitting under the watchful eye of another police officer. "We'll get to the bottom of this, Maddie. But right now, we need to talk to Warner. Something tells me he knows more than he's letting on."

"Good luck with that," I muttered, feeling a surge of anger. James had charmed his way into everyone's lives, convinced Stanton Collier to invest in some wild goose chase, and now here we were—one man dead, a woman in the hospital, and the whole town whispering about lost Confederate treasure. "He's a snake."

Allen gave me a wry smile. "Snakes are my specialty."

I followed him inside the inn. James Warner lounged in one of the red wingback chairs in the parlor, looking more like a lazy guest than a man with murder hanging over his head. His eyes flicked over to me as we entered, but he quickly turned his attention back to Allen.

"Detective," he said, voice smooth as silk. "I don't see why all this fuss is necessary. I've already told you everything I know."

Allen raised an eyebrow. "Have you? Because I'm not sure you've told us about the fraud charges from a few years back."

James stiffened, his smile faltered for just a second. "That was all a misunderstanding."

"Right," Allen drawled, pulling up a chair and sitting across from him. "You misunderstand a lot of things, don't you? Like getting rich off other people's money. You've got quite the record, Mr. Warner."

I couldn't resist chiming in. "And now you've got a man dead."

James shot me a sharp look. "I didn't kill Stanton, and I had nothing to do with that housekeeper. I'm just as much a victim here as anyone else."

"Victim, huh?" Allen leaned forward. "So why don't you tell us what you were doing out in the barn the night Stanton was shot?"

James hesitated, his smooth image cracking for just a moment. "I ... I was just looking. The Colliers were interested in the legend, okay? I thought maybe we could strike gold, so to speak."

"And what about the tunnels?" I asked, stepping closer, my anger rising. "Did you know about them? Did you use them?"

His eyes flickered nervously, but he shook his head. "No. I swear, I don't know anything about tunnels."

Allen stood up, looming over James. "Well, you're still a suspect. I suggest you keep yourself available while we investigate. And don't even think about running. We'll be watching."

James paled but said nothing as Allen motioned for him to leave. The minute he was out the door, I felt my anger simmering.

"I don't like this," I said, pacing the room. "He's lying. I just know it. He knows something."

Allen nodded, rubbing the back of his neck. "Yeah, I'm sure he does.

But until we get more evidence, all we've got is circumstantial. And as much as I want to throw him in a cell, we need to play this smart."

"I just want him out of here," I muttered. "Out from under my roof … I don't trust him. He'll be sneaking around."

"I'll have an officer stationed here tonight," Allen reassured me. "But we need to keep digging."

"Digging? Please don't use that term," I said with a laugh.

Just then, Allen's phone rang. He answered it, frowning as he listened. "Okay, I'll be right there."

He hung up and looked at me, his expression serious. "Sally's awake. Chief Barlow is trying to get her to confess."

"Confess to what? She's a victim in this mess. Wait a minute. What about the results of your forensic tests? You promised me you'd share the report. Does it implicate Sally?" I asked.

"We found her fingerprints on the gun case, however I was ready to write that off what with her being the housekeeper and likely had dusted the cabinet. We matched one print to the Remington's hilt but the other prints on the handle and trigger were smudged. The revolver was definitely the murder weapon; ballistics matched the bullets."

"So you're saying Chief Barlow thinks she's guilty of murder? I can't believe that."

I thought of the dark tunnel stretching beneath the inn, feeling a chill creep up my spine. Whoever was behind this wasn't finished yet. They murdered Stanton Collier and would have allowed Sally Rawlins to die in those dank tunnels—and for what? A unproven fabled cache of Confederate gold.

"We need to search our basement and find the connecting door to those tunnels," I said, my voice shaking.

"I'm positive Warner was part of this caper, but I don't think he was working alone," Allen said.

I pushed my hair back behind my ears as I paced the room. It didn't feel right. There was no way that Sally shot Stanton or tied herself up, yet James Warner labeled as the killer seemed too easy. He made the perfect patsy.

"As much as it pains me to say this, I don't think James Warner killed Stanton Collier. I believe him. Oh, I'm sure he's guilty of trying to swindle the Collier family and maybe even the Beauregards, but murder ...? What person is stupid enough to kill another and then hang around? Warner isn't that stupid."

"You may be right. Only in the movies do cases solve themselves this quickly. I plan on speaking with Sally, maybe she knows more than she's letting on and I'll confirm her alibi for the time when Collier was shot."

⬣◆⬣

"Oh Grannie! What am I going to do?" I cried as I stared at the family portraits atop the fireplace mantle.

"You're already doing it. Just protect what you hold dear and don't be afraid of the truth," Grannie said as her image shimmered in the afternoon light.

"Did you know about a secret tunnel between the barn and the house? I'm afraid to search the basement for fear of what I'll find. I'm so confused and scared. What if the murderer is still hiding there?"

"No sugar, I didn't. Don't be afraid. I assure you, the house is empty except for that young man upstairs."

"Okay. Thank you Grannie. I guess I feel a bit better knowing you aren't detecting any other energy in the house."

I turned away from the mantle as Allen tromped into the living room.

"There you are! Are you ready to do this? Let's see if we can find where that tunnel opens into the basement of this place."

"You know, I've lived here all my life. When I was a little kid, I'd go downstairs with Grannie and the basement always felt spooky but now ... I'm positively creeped out by the thought of it and the idea someone could have entered my home unseen." I took a deep swallow and straightened my shoulders then looked at Allen. "Okay. I'm ready."

I picked up my flashlight, tested to make sure it still lit, then led Allen to the basement door next to the kitchen pantry. I eased the door open, paused to listen, then turned on the light switch.

"Want me to go first?" he asked as he watched my hand shake.

"Um ... maybe you better." I turned sideways so he could slide past me and we started down the wooden stairs. My right hand grasped the railing as my left held the flashlight with trembling fingers.

The damp, moldy smell hit my nose the moment we reached the bottom step. It felt like I was back in the tunnel. Crumbling stucco covered the outer walls. This basement was centuries old. Every inch of it seemed to whisper with the weight of forgotten secrets, and family belongings packed away and forgotten from decades ago.

Pipes and heating ducts crisscrossed the ceiling under the upper floor rafters. Two fifty-gallon hot water heaters stood side-by-side in a corner to provide enough hot water to guests. A large gas furnace that we had modernized five years ago occupied floor space next to them. Cobwebs hung above our heads and dust coated shelving. A row of empty mason jars filled a tall shelf. I recalled when they were full, fruits of Grannie's labors making her own pickles and canning the cucumbers and tomatoes from our garden patch.

We moved slowly about the space. The basement covered the entire width and length of the farmhouse but had been partitioned into two rooms years ago. We started exploring the main room on the left. I directed my flashlight onto a workbench and fishing gear. Three of Granddaddy Charles' rods and reels hung on hooks. His lores and fish hooks filled recycled coffee tins. My mind flashed to images of him sitting on a tall stool, painstakingly wrapping wisps of feathers onto tiny lores.

I poked into plastic tubs filled with old fabric and notions then pushed aside cardboard boxes that had absorbed so much moisture they felt damp to the touch.

As I moved a box sitting on top of a rusted metal cabinet, an image rose before me. I screamed.

Allen rushed to my side. "What is it?" he asked as he wrapped a comforting arm about my shoulders and directed his light into the darker corner.

"Oh good gracious," I breathed a sigh of relief. My stalker turned out to be a mannequin dress form. I swear my heart had jumped into my throat.

Allen laughed out loud. "Appears harmless enough."

"Oh you!" I brushed his arm off my shoulders and turned away, mortified by my reaction.

"Let's keep looking, okay?" he asked.

"We've got to keep looking. I won't feel secure sleeping in this house until we do. The door to the hidden tunnel is down here somewhere."

We continued to walk among the boxes and pieces of old furniture and myriad of items stored over the years. A layer of dust covered everything. I had to remind myself not to touch my face or I'd look like a clown. I already felt grimy just being in the subterranean cellar.

"You're awfully quiet," Allen muttered, flashing his light across the old wooden beams overhead. "You usually have more to say when we're investigating."

"I'm thinking," I replied, quickening my pace to keep up with him. "And trying to avoid tripping over all this stuff. My mind keeps replaying Lionel finding that rusty skeleton key."

The previous night, Lionel had burst through the kitchen door, holding up a piece of old metal. "Maddie! Allen! You've got to see this! C'mon."

"I thought I told you to stay out of that root cellar and wait on me to search," Allen chastised.

We all rushed back to the root cellar, where Lionel had been searching through the underground tunnels. He led us down the ladder, excitement radiating off him.

"I found this buried near where we found Sally," he explained, holding out the metal piece. He pointed to a place where he had loosened soil at the corner of a rusty shelf.

Allen took it, turning it over in his hands. It was a rusted key. "Where does this go?"

"No idea," Lionel said. "But it was hidden pretty well. Maybe there's a stronghold box or something connected to those missing Confederate coins."

"Lionel, you've got to stop thinking about Confederate money that doesn't exist," I had warned him.

And now, here we were exploring the recesses of the inn's basement, hoping to find just that or at least a secret hidden door connecting to the root cellar and outside.

Allen shot me a half-smile. "Don't go keeping secrets from me, Maddie. I can tell when you've got something on your mind."

If only he knew. Grannie's voice had been in my ear since the moment we crossed into the basement, her familiar drawl like a whisper on the wind.

"He's looking in the wrong places, Maddie-girl," she said. *"You know these walls better than he does. Follow your instincts."*

I clenched my jaw, not responding aloud, though it was tempting. Allen was already suspicious of me, always picking up on when I had a private conversation with my ghostly grandmother. And I wasn't about to explain that to him. He'd be ready to commit me for psychiatric care if he knew I spoke with a ghost.

The beam of his flashlight suddenly caught something—footprints in the dust leading into the other side. Fresh ones.

"Look at this," Allen said, stooping down to examine them. "Some-one's been down here recently."

Chapter Nine

Phantom Gold

I knelt next to him, my breath catching in my throat. The prints were small, definitely not the size of a man's foot. They led into a corner of the divided basement, right where an old steamer trunk sat, half-buried under cobwebs. I stepped back as Allen crouched down to get a closer look.

"Grannie! Have you seen this trunk before?" I whispered. I shot a quick glance at Allen to see if he had heard me, but he was preoccupied with the trunk and lock mechanism.

"No sugar. I don't know where that came from," Grannie replied as she floated over the scene.

"That's got to be it," I directed my comment to Allen, speaking in a low voice as if someone might overhear me. "The key Lionel found might go to that trunk."

Allen pulled the rusty key from his pocket and handed it to me. "Why don't you do the honors?"

My hand shook a little as I tried the key in the lock. It fit. I jiggled the key and twisted it hard before it turned with a soft *click,* then I lifted the lid. Inside contained a sprinkling of sand, an old moth-eaten wool blanket—and a single gold coin.

Allen reached for it, rubbing the coin between his fingers. "This looks like Confederate gold."

I stared at it, my heart sinking. Pulling the blanket out of the chest confirmed it, nothing else. Only one coin.

"One lousy coin ... a man died because of one coin? Well, that's it then. Lionel will be very disappointed."

"We don't know for sure that Collier was murdered because of the treasure. There could be another reason," Allen said.

Obviously, the legendary treasure everyone had whispered about wasn't here. The empty trunk made that clear.

"You're close," Grannie's voice echoed softly in my ear. *"But you need to look deeper."*

Look deeper where? Why was she so cryptic? Did she want me to find the secret tunnel door or was there really a fortune to be found?

"Maddie?" Allen's voice broke my concentration. He was staring at me, suspicion etched into his features. "You okay?"

I forced a smile. "Yes, just disappointed. I thought we had found an answer. Maybe there's more treasure hidden in the tunnel, if we can find the entrance."

His eyes narrowed slightly. "Thought you didn't believe in the gold? You said the rumors were false." He gave me a hard look then switched gears. "Sally knew about this trunk, didn't she? She had access to the barn and knew her way around this property. You can't honestly believe she's innocent."

I stood up, pushing back my frustration. I couldn't believe the unexpected track his mind took. Whatever happened to the rule of innocent until proven guilty?

"I don't know if Sally saw this trunk or not, but I do know that Sally didn't kill Stanton Collier. She's just not capable, Allen. You're looking in the wrong direction. You need to concentrate on who had motive to murder Collier."

"And you're too close to the situation," he countered, standing up to face me. "You're Sally's friend. I understand you've gotten close since she came to the inn. Maybe you're not seeing things clearly."

My temper flared, but I tried to keep my voice steady. We squared off, facing one another, each refusing to give in. Sparks flew.

"I'm seeing things just fine. What about Susan Harper? She's been hovering around Stephen since day one and acting suspicious. Or Hugh Beauregard, who's got a reputation for getting himself tangled in debts he can't pay off. Maybe you're letting family relationships color your opinion. Either of them could have had a motive."

Allen sighed, running a hand through his hair. "That's a low blow, Maddie. Give me credit for being more professional than that. I put aside my family ties. I'm not saying we don't investigate Susan and even Uncle Hugh ... but right now, the Chief likes Sally for this. She had access to the barn and the house. She may even have helped in this treasure hunt—"

"And I'm saying she didn't do it," I interrupted, my voice sharper than I intended. "You're just being stubborn ... so sure you've got the right person. Well, you don't. There's more going on here, Allen. We need to look deeper." I ground my teeth and threw up my hands.

The tension between us crackled, heavier than the air in that musty basement. I knew Allen was just doing his job, but I couldn't let him pin this murder on Sally when I felt deep down that she was innocent.

He turned away, scanning the walls with his flashlight. "Fine. We'll keep looking. But I'm not letting this go, Maddie. If Sally had a part in this, I'm going to find out."

I followed him, my headache building, pounding with frustration. We both slowly investigated the concrete walls, running our hands across the rough surfaces. After tracing one wall, we moved to another.

Grannie's voice guided me toward a section of the basement wall that seemed oddly discolored. *"I feel an aura of energy here."*

I hesitated before running my hand along the stone. There—a faint seam in the wall. It has to be the hidden door.

"Allen! Look at this."

"Push it, Maddie," Grannie whispered.

I did as she said, pressing gently. A hinge creaked. The door sprung open, revealing the entrance to the tunnel. Dust swirled in the air, and a musty draft hit my face.

"Maddie!" Allen spun around as the hidden door opened. "How did you—"

"Guess I've got better instincts than you give me credit for," I said with a small smirk, trying to lighten the mood.

Allen stepped closer, his expression unreadable. "You're a mystery, Maddie Brooke."

I met his gaze. "You have no idea."

And with that, we stepped into the tunnel together; the darkness swallowed us whole. I reached for Allen's hand as we blindly explored the path toward the central root cellar where I had found Sally.

Rough stone walls, only six feet high, created a narrow passageway. Twice, Allen had to stoop to prevent banging his head on low beams as we inched forward. Our flashlights produced narrow ribbons of light to guide our footsteps in the close confines. Finally, I spotted the gap that opened into the wider root cellar where shelving stood against the walls holding old jars filled with decayed substances. The chair where Sally had been tied lay on its side, knocked over by police officers previously documenting the scene.

We found no evidence of any mysterious treasure chest or bags of Confederate gold within the underground vault. Our fortune hunting for phantom gold came up empty. Allen glanced around then retraced his steps back to the hidden door and snapped pictures with his cell phone. Studying the portal, he ran his hand along the frame and ledge above. A smile curved his lips as his fingers touched a wooden lever above the doorframe.

"I found something that springs this door open. Check this out," he called to me as I stepped back into the tunnel.

Allen pressed the door closed. I watched as his hand pulled on a wooden trigger and the door slowly released. Its frame stood ajar a few inches, enough for a person's fingertips to grasp and pull wider.

My hand flew to my mouth as I stared at the tricky mechanism.

"Do you think this secret passage was built when the house was erected? I can't believe my family never knew of its existence," I said as we closed the door again and I played with the trigger to test it again.

"Considering how it connects to the basement and the distance between the house and the trap door behind the barn, I'd say this is probably original to the date of construction. Did you say it was 1830? Seems like this hidden tunnel would have come in handy for runaway slaves or maybe it was used by smugglers."

"Smugglers? Hardly. I could imagine that premise if Magnolia Blossom resided in a seaport community, like Savannah or Charleston. Somehow, I doubt there were smugglers in the mountain regions. You Yankees must think all Southerners are thieves or moonshine bootleggers." I shot him a scathing look.

Allen grimaced as he turned back into the main root cellar. "Let's not start a North versus South argument. I merely speculated on the reasons for building something like this."

"Well, if the house were older, I'd guess that the tunnel could have been an escape route from Indian attacks. But 1830 ... I think the Monacan Indian tribes that populated the Shenandoah and Blue Ridge had left the territory way before that date. The Cherokee Nation still lived in the Blue Ridge until 1836 but more in North Carolina and Tennessee than Virginia, at least they did until Andrew Jackson's terrible treaty and the Trail of Tears resettlement."

"Wow, you really were a history major," Allen said with a laugh.

"Sorry. Too much information? Touchy subject with me. Yes, my history studies encompassed the colonial years and the settlement of this region by both whites and Indians. I'd like to think that my ancestors treated their Indian neighbors with respect and kindness. The American Indian certainly deserved better than what history recorded."

"Mm-hmm. Which brings us back to the present day purpose of

this hidden tunnel. Based upon the footprints in your basement and Sally's capture, I'd say the tunnel has been used by criminals."

"I don't suppose it would do any good to try and lift fingerprints from that door thing," I stated more than inquired.

"No. Rough wood, prints won't adhere to that. I will take photographs and impressions of the footprints on the basement floor. That might lead to our suspect," Allen said. "C'mon, let's get out of here and go back through the house. With your permission, I'd like to seal off the outer trap door and dismantle this door latch to prevent anyone entering these tunnels and accessing the house."

"Yes, absolutely! You can start by taking away the ladder under that trap door. I'll ask Tom to seal it from the outside and cover it in dirt again. Maybe Tom can figure out a way to nail shut the basement door too, just to be sure."

"Okay. Sounds like a plan," Allen said as he pulled down the ladder and laid it on the floor then we squeezed through the secret door into the basement.

Allen took a hammer to the trigger mechanism, disabling it. If there was any living thing or person in that secret cellar now, they'd be trapped for eternity.

The pieces of the puzzle started falling into place. The hidden passage. The cellar. This was how the murderer had escaped after killing Stanton. He'd slipped away unnoticed, disappearing into the under-ground network that connected the barn to the inn. The question was ... who had known about it?

Chapter Ten

Interrogation

The room smelled of lemon-scented disinfectant. I sat on the hard plastic chair by Sally Rawlins' hospital bed, my notebook open in my lap, pen poised, ready to catch any slip-up she might make. Across the room, Maddie sat perched on the edge of the small armchair, her gaze unwavering as she watched over her housekeeper like a hawk. She hadn't said a word since we walked in, but I knew the tension between us still lingered from our argument in the basement. Sally had been through a lot, and Maddie felt fiercely protective of her. But I couldn't let that cloud my judgment. There were too many questions that needed answering, and Sally might be the only one who could fill in the gaps.

Sally lay back against the raised bed, her face pale but alert. She squinted and shaded her eyes with her hand from the piercing sunlight pouring through the window. Fresh bandages wrapped the head wound and around her wrists, the rope burns visible on her arms. She looked fragile in the thin hospital gown, but there was a steely determination in her eyes.

I adjusted the window blinds to slightly darken the room. Sally lowered her hand from her eyes. I turned to her as I claimed my seat again.

"Better? You okay to talk?" I asked, keeping my voice steady, neutral. I didn't want to push too hard or too fast. Sally had been through enough already. But time was running out, and I needed answers.

She nodded, her voice shaky. "I'll do my best, Detective."

"Good," I said, leaning forward slightly, trying to make the atmosphere less confrontational. "Let's start simple. Tell me what happened the night you went missing."

Sally shifted uncomfortably, her hands fidgeting in her lap. Her fingers twisted a corner of the lightweight blanket draped across the bed. Sally's eyes darted about the sterile hospital room with its celery green walls and scuffed vinyl flooring. The usual framed patient notices and bland art prints hung on the walls. Next to her bed, several machines beeped quietly with blinking lights, monitoring her heart rate, blood pressure, and respiratory rates, along with other standard vital signs. A myriad of cords linked the monitors to her bed and the sensors taped to her chest and arm. Sally raised a hand to swipe a lock of hair from her eyes; the purple bruise on the back of her hand gave evidence of the I.V. needle inserted earlier into her vein.

Maddie shot her an encouraging smile but didn't say anything. I appreciated her silence, even if it made me feel like I was the bad guy in the room.

"I—" Sally hesitated, her voice cracking. "I didn't know it would turn out like this. I swear. James Warner came to me a few days before the wedding. Said he was onto something big, something to do with a treasure hunt."

"Treasure hunt?" I raised an eyebrow, playing dumb, even though we both knew what she was talking about. I wanted her to explain it, to hear her version of the story.

"Yes," she said, swallowing hard. "He said there were old Confederate coins hidden somewhere on the property. That Maddie's family was rich and had some kind of connection to it. He told me it was just a harmless search for treasure, that no one would get hurt."

"And you believed him?" I asked, trying to keep the skepticism out of my voice.

Sally nodded, guilt clouding her eyes. "I thought it was just a prank at first, honestly. I didn't think ... well, I didn't think anything bad would happen. He told me I'd get a share of the money. I'm broke. That's why I'm working as a housekeeper. I needed that money."

"And what was your role in all of this?" I leaned in a little closer, keeping my gaze steady on her. "What exactly did you do for James?"

She looked down at her hands, her fingers twisting nervously in the blanket. "I ... I unlocked the barn and the shed for him. That's all I did. He told me he needed a shovel to dig. I knew Tom kept his gardening tools there. It seemed harmless. He said it was all part of the search."

I pressed her for more details and to prove my forensic evidence. I leaned toward her and kept my voice level.

"What about the gun case in Maddie's study? Did you unlock that for Warner? Your fingerprints are on the glass. Did you take out a revolver and kill Stanton Collier?"

Sally burst into tears, shaking her head from side to side. "No ... no! You've got to believe me I had nothing to do with his death. I did find the key in the desk drawer, but I gave it to Tom to open the display case and for him to show Mr. Collier and the groom's father, Mr. Beauregard, the weapons."

"All right, Sally. Let's talk about where Maddie found you. Did you go into the tunnels with James?" I asked, my tone a little sharper than I intended.

Sally shook her head vehemently, her eyes wide. "No. No, I didn't even know about the tunnels until you found me."

"Why did you write that note? Sally, had you planned on running away with your reward?"

"I got scared. Mr. Collier had been shot and then I overheard James talking with somebody about keeping all the money for himself. He sounded angry. I decided to hide, but when I tried to leave by the kitchen door, someone hit me over the head. They blindfolded me and carried me ... wherever they took me. All I remember was waking up to a damp smell and silence. I had no idea where I was. I thought I was all alone until I heard distant voices."

A tap on the door interrupted me. I looked up to see Maddie's friend Lily in a white lab coat with her stethoscope looped on her shoulder. She nodded to me and shot Maddie a smile.

"Everything okay in here?" Lily asked, her focus on Sally. She walked over to the bed, glanced at the monitor readings, read the patient chart then turned to go. "I'll check on you later."

Sally nodded and gave the doctor a slight smile.

I glanced at Maddie. She sat perfectly still, her lips pressed together in a thin line, her finger tangled in a lock of hair ... I could see the worry in her eyes. She wanted to believe Sally, but even she had to be questioning how deep her involvement went. I turned my attention back to Sally and began my questioning again.

"So, James Warner and someone else took you down there?" I pressed. "Did you ever hear or see this other person?"

"No," she whispered, her voice trembling now. "I never saw them. Someone blindfolded me and tied my hands the whole time. But I could hear them talking. The other person, the voice ... it sounded different, like with an accent. I don't know. Not like ours, more northern maybe? It was muffled. I'm not sure." Tears filled her eyes as she rested her head against the pillows.

My mind immediately went to Hugh Beauregard, the groom's father. He was the only male left on the property, except he came from old Southern money. He didn't have a northern accent, but he'd be interested in finding gold. It didn't quite fit. Still, it was a lead worth following.

"And what about the gold coins?" I asked, watching her reaction carefully. "We found one in the steamer trunk in the basement. Did you know anything about that?"

Her eyes widened, and she looked genuinely confused. "Gold coins?

You mean the treasure was real? I didn't know anything about that trunk, I swear."

I stared at her, trying to decide if she was telling the truth. Her reaction seemed real, but I'd seen enough people lie to know that appearances could be deceiving.

"Sally, whose footprints were in the basement?" I asked, my voice softer now. "We found fresh prints in the dust leading to that trunk. Were they yours?"

She shook her head, her face pale. "No, they weren't mine. I've never been down there. I ... I know the house has a basement but I've never needed to go down there. The kitchen pantry holds everything I need to clean the house."

Maddie finally spoke up, her voice calm but firm. "Allen, she's telling the truth. I know Sally never entered the basement. Sally's never been involved in anything like this before. She's certainly not capable of hurting anyone." Maddie glared at me then reached for Sally's hand, offering her sympathetic support.

I shot Maddie a glance, my jaw tightening. I knew she wanted to protect her employee, but I couldn't let my guard down. Not yet.

"I believe you didn't know things would go this far," I said to Sally, keeping my tone measured. "But you have to understand, this is serious. A man is dead. And you were involved, whether you meant to be or not."

Tears welled up in Sally's eyes, and her hands clenched Maddie's hands tightly. "I didn't want to see anyone get hurt, Detective. I just ... I just wanted a chance for a new beginning. James promised me a share of the treasure. He said we'd all be rich."

"And now you're lucky to be alive," I said bluntly. "Whoever was working with James clearly didn't have your best interests at heart."

She nodded, tears spilling down her cheeks now. "I know. I know I was stupid. If it wasn't for Maddie, I could have died down there and no one would have known or cared. But I didn't kill Mr. Collier. I swear."

Her monitor beeped and lights flashed as her blood pressure line spiked then settled back down.

I sighed, running a hand through my hair. It was hard not to feel sorry for her, but I couldn't let emotions cloud the facts.

"I'm going to look into James Warner and this partner of his," I said, standing up and slipping my notebook back into my pocket. "But if you remember anything else—anything at all—you need to tell me. Understand?"

Sally nodded quickly, wiping her eyes. "I will. I promise."

Maddie stood as well, placing a comforting hand on Sally's shoulder. "We'll figure this out, Sally. Just focus on getting better."

Sally nodded and smiled timidly. "Thank you Maddie, for believing in me. I'm sorry I caused you trouble."

As we left the room, Maddie fell into step beside me, her arms crossed tightly over her chest. I could feel the tension radiating off her, but I didn't say anything at first. We were both lost in our thoughts.

Finally, she broke the silence. "Allen, do you really think Sally could have killed Stanton Collier?"

I shrugged, glancing at her sideways. "It's possible. But honestly, I think she's more of a pawn in all this. James Warner's the one we need to dig into."

Maddie frowned, her eyes narrowing. "And what about the other person? The one with the accent?"

"That's what I'm trying to figure out," I said, my voice grim. "If Sally's telling the truth—and I think she is—then there's someone else involved. Someone who's still out there."

Maddie's face was pale, her eyes full of worry. "You think they'll come back? Am I in danger at the inn? We closed off the tunnel and hidden door; they can't get back in that way. Should I lock my doors to any inn guests? James Warner checked out this morning. I was happy to see him go and now after listening to Sally, even more so. She definitely confirmed our suspicions that he was involved. If anyone killed Collier, he appears to be the guilty party, despite my previous doubts. Who else could it be?"

I didn't want to scare her, but I couldn't lie either. "You need to be on guard. It's possible these people could come back. Especially if they think more treasure's still hidden somewhere."

Maddie was silent for a moment, then she shook her head. "Grannie always said lusting after treasure was ill-gotten gains. Look at what a single gold coin has caused."

I smiled slightly, despite the tension. "Your Grannie might've been right."

We walked in silence for a few more steps before I spoke again. "Look, I know you want to protect Sally. But I've got to follow the evidence. If something points to her ..."

"I know," Maddie interrupted, her voice tight. "But just ... keep an open mind, okay? There's more going on here than what we can see."

I nodded, but my mind was already racing ahead, piecing together the fragments of the puzzle. One thing was clear—this wasn't just about a treasure hunt gone wrong. There was something much darker lurking beneath the surface. And we were just starting to scratch it.

Chapter Eleven

Friends

The sun dipped low behind the Blue Ridge Mountains, casting a warm, golden glow over the rolling hills and magnolia trees surrounding the Magnolia Blossom Inn. We had claimed our favorite spot on the wide veranda, where the scent of honeysuckle and magnolias mingled with the cool evening air. The soft creak of the wooden boards beneath our chairs provided a familiar, homey rhythm, while Luke and Prissy hovered near our feet, their eyes locked on the platter of fancy cheese snacks Tom had whipped up. Every time Tom experimented with a new recipe, my taste buds and appetite always benefited. This was one of those times. I didn't mind being a human guinea pig at all when it came to Tom's culinary treats.

"One more sniff from you, Luke, and I'm getting you your own cheese tray," I said, laughing as I nudged the dog's eager nose away from the table. He gave me those soulful eyes that said, *But Mom, that's what I had in mind* and laid down with a dramatic sigh.

Prissy, on the other hand, sat prim and proper on the edge of Lionel's chair, her eyes narrowed as she inspected every morsel with the intensity of a jewel thief.

"Prissy, darling, you're not getting any Brie," Lionel said, shooing her away gently. "It's far too sophisticated for your uncultured palate."

The cat shot him a withering look, then sauntered over to Lily, her backup source for treats.

I took a sip of my wine cocktail—a crisp mix of white wine and elderflower liqueur that Lionel had concocted—and leaned back, enjoying the peace of the moment. Well, the relative peace. The murder of Stanton Collier still hung over us like a dark cloud, but for now, on the veranda with my best friends and a platter of Tom's gourmet appetizers, I could pretend everything was just a little bit normal.

"Lionel, I feel so guilty keeping you from your work at the Center. Hope I'm not getting you in trouble for neglecting your duties. How's Attorney Warner, by the way?" I asked as I reclined against the rocker.

"Who says I'm neglecting my work? I'll have you know that as long as my laptop is nearby, I'm connected to my office. Don't worry, I'm staying on top of things. If I wasn't able to do that, I wouldn't be here. Funny you ask about Lee, he just asked me about you the other day; wanted to make sure you were doing well with the new party venue. Lee says he approves the new advertising," Lionel replied, reaching for another tasty morsel.

"What new advertising?" I asked and stared at Lionel until he broke into a wide grin.

"Hmm, could be the online spread I pushed out with photos of the barn and wedding décor ... before the whole shooting incident, of course. It's on your web page and Facebook plus I might have posted an ad on Google. You should get inquiry calls soon."

I shook my head in wonder. Lionel, in his quiet way, had created a marketing blitz for the inn and didn't tell me. I reached across and squeezed his hand, mouthing a silent thank you. He merely smiled in return.

"Okay, I'm just going to say it," Lily began, pushing her half-empty glass toward the center of the table. "I feel much better now that hidden passage is sealed off. I was worried to death while y'all played Indiana Jones down there. Of course if you hadn't, poor Sally might still be tied up and left for dead down there. Another soul to haunt the inn. Makes me shudder to think of that. How did the interrogation go with Sally and Allen this morning? Did you learn anything new?"

"I think the only thing either of us learned was confirmation James Warner had been involved in the search for the treasure and that he had an accomplice. Sally said two people carried her into the tunnel after hitting her on the head. Poor Sally. James misled her into helping him but I think that was the extent of it. I'm sure."

"Is she certain two people carried her into the cellar? I mean, how does she know if she was knocked unconscious?" Lily asked.

"She told Allen she heard two voices talking. I guess she concluded that two people carried her, but you're right ... one person could have carried her down there. Maybe she heard them talking later." Now I began to rethink our original theory. Hmm.

"Can't imagine how she felt being down there all alone. That spooky tunnel felt haunted all right and we weren't there that long," Lionel said, waving a piece of cheese in the air. "I could sense it. That place had the energy of, like, a thousand Civil War-era ghosts."

"You're being overly dramatic. But there was definitely one ghost there," I said, giving him a knowing smile. "Grannie wasn't shy about making her presence known while Allen and I investigated the basement. I wouldn't have found the hidden door without her."

Lionel shuddered dramatically. "That old woman—rest her spectral soul—nearly gave me a heart attack. One minute I'm poking around in the dust, and the next, she's right there, hovering over my shoulder like it's her personal job to monitor my every move."

A soft breeze stirred, and I swear I felt the temperature drop a few degrees. *"Lionel, dear,"* came Grannie's unmistakable voice from behind us. *"You'd best remember who owns this property. I'm simply ensuring no one damages what's rightfully mine."*

Lionel jumped, nearly spilling his drink, while Lily and I exchanged amused glances.

"Speak of the devil," Lionel muttered under his breath, though he offered Grannie a polite nod. "You know, it wouldn't hurt to knock or something before you just … appear."

Grannie chuckled, her transparent figure shimmering in the fading light as she floated onto the veranda. *"Knock? What's the point of being a ghost if I have to knock? Besides, you three were getting a bit too comfortable, and I wanted to remind you there's still work to be done."*

"I don't know, Grannie," I said, reaching for another cracker topped with some kind of fancy cheese I couldn't pronounce. "We've been chasing clues all over this inn, and what do we have to show for it? One rusty trunk, a secret tunnel that looks like it was used by bootleggers, and a single gold coin. It just proves my theory that this Confederate fortune is a hoax."

Lily nodded in agreement, folding her arms across her chest. "I have to agree. Honestly, I'm wondering if this treasure ever existed. That one coin could've just been a fluke, right?"

"Or it's part of a larger stash," Lionel countered, his eyes gleaming with excitement. "I mean, think about it—why else would James Warner and his mysterious accomplice be so interested in digging around here? There's got to be more."

I sighed, leaning back in my chair. "That's what worries me. James is still out there, and who knows what he's up to. And then there's Hugh Beauregard, Stephen's father … something about that man just doesn't sit right with me. You'd think he'd be more upset for his son, what with the wedding postponed and everything. What does that make him?"

"Yeah, he's a cold fish—slick," Lionel echoed, adopting a mock-serious tone. "Darling, I'll tell you who is slick, it's that Susan Harper. The woman has 'snake in the grass' written all over her. I watched her over the weekend and I swear she acted odd. I caught her twice snooping in parts of the house where she had no business being."

"I don't know," Lily said thoughtfully. "I observed her and Susan seemed more ... desperate than evil. It's like she was playing a part she wasn't very good at, and she was hoping no one noticed."

"Desperate or not, she's got motive," I pointed out. "If she's in love with Stephen, then maybe she was trying to break up the wedding. Stanton Collier might have been in the way. What if Susan thought Stephen would turn to her if his chances for Collier wealth no longer existed?"

"That's kind of a convoluted theory," Lily remarked as she sipped her wine cocktail.

"Or Hugh Beauregard," Lionel said, raising an eyebrow. "If he'd been banking on that marriage for the Collier money, then maybe Stanton wasn't moving fast enough with the deal. Old money types can be brutal when they feel like their family legacy is at stake."

"Well, Hugh certainly has that air about him," Lily added, her voice tinged with sarcasm. "Like he's living in some grand Southern novel where he's the hero, saving the family estate from ruin. But it would have been foolish of him to kill the golden goose before the marriage took place. Wouldn't it have made more sense to see his son married to Savannah first and let her inherit her father's fortune?"

"You've made a good point," I said.

Grannie, who had been listening intently, chimed in. *"You young folks overcomplicate things. People kill for much simpler reasons—greed, jealousy, fear. It doesn't have to be some elaborate scheme."*

"Thank you for the insight, Grannie," Lionel said with a dramatic bow. "Always good to know we're not looking for some evil genius here."

Grannie's ghostly form shimmered again, her eyes twinkling with amusement. *"Just keep your wits about you, that's all I'm saying."*

Prissy leapt onto the table and sniffed at the cheese plate again, but Lionel quickly snatched it away. "Prissy, please. Cheese is for humans. You've got your fancy gourmet cat food inside."

The little black and white cat responded by batting at his hand, clearly unimpressed by his cheese-snobbery.

I took a sip of my cocktail, savoring the light, fruity taste. "All jokes aside, I keep coming back to that trunk in the basement. Why would someone go to all the trouble of sealing it up, only to leave one gold coin inside?"

"Maybe it's a message," Lionel said, popping another piece of cheese into his mouth. "Like, 'Hey, you found one, but good luck finding the rest.'"

"Or it's a warning," Lily added. "Like, 'This is all you're getting, so stop looking.'"

"Either way, it's not over," I said, my tone growing serious. "Whoever's involved in this won't stop until they get what they want. Whether it's gold, revenge, or something else entirely, we need to be ready for whatever comes next."

"So what's next?" Lionel asked.

"Hmm, I think we need to learn as much as we can about Susan Harper and maybe both Hugh and Stephen Beauregard. It doesn't hurt to have as much information as possible to know who or what we're dealing with."

Grannie nodded approvingly, her voice soft but firm. *"That's the spirit, Maddie. Stay sharp and remember—you've got more allies than you think."*

I smiled, feeling a bit more at ease despite the looming mystery. With Grannie's watchful eye, Lionel's quick wit, and Lily's practical wisdom, I knew we'd figure this out. And as the sun finally slipped behind the horizon, casting long shadows over the veranda, I couldn't help but feel like we were one step closer to uncovering the truth.

"Well, I don't know about y'all," Lionel said, stretching his arms above his head, "but I could use a refill. Who's up for another round?"

I raised my glass, grinning. "Count me in."

Lily laughed, leaning back in her chair. "Why not? We might as well enjoy the calm before the storm."

Prissy meowed in agreement, and Luke wagged his tail, clearly hoping for one last morsel of food.

As we clinked our glasses together, the tension from the last few days seemed to lift, if only for a little while. But deep down, I knew the mystery wasn't over yet—and that the answers we were looking for were still out there, waiting to be found.

Chapter Twelve

Condolences

"Thanks for coming with me to this. I know it's not exactly a fun event, attending a funeral service, but I appreciate your support. With Stanton dying at the inn and everyone else staying as our guests, it's only proper Southern manners to attend and show my respects," I told Lionel and Lily. We walked toward the massive entrance doors of the Woodhill Funeral Home in Charlottesville.

Woodhill's sleek architectural style with glass panels and sharp angles gave the appearance of a major corporate business center rather than a place for memorial observances. Inside, the décor stressed shades of gray, ranging from light silver to pewter on the furnishings and wall coverings. The wide lobby held multiple doors leading into separate visitation rooms. Two of the four doors stood open; a placard rested on a tall easel next to each door. It contained a picture and the name of the deceased. A lectern held a guest book for visitors to sign.

We waited in a slow-moving line to approach the visitation room for Stanton Collier. When it was my turn, I signed the guest book then took a second to scan the signatures for names I might know. My eyes widened as I read Allen Crawford's bold scroll near the top of the page. I instantly craned my neck to search the crowd for his tall figure, but didn't spot him among all the other suits.

Throngs of people stood speaking softly or shuffling around to greet others they hadn't seen in ages or not since the last corporate event, because that's what this felt like. Business associates, people in the electronics industry, shareholders, even a journalist or two crowded the room. Over-powering waves of heavy colognes and summer sweat from over a hundred people mixed with sweet floral scents radiating from the adjoining room. Multiple baskets displayed heady arrangements of roses, carnations, lilies, and asters tucked into sprays of green foliage. The combined fragrances clung to the faintly ventilated atmosphere.

Lily and Lionel walked next to me as we made our way through the crowd toward the front of the room. Several rows of folding chairs had been set up on the plush slate-colored carpeting in the middle of the spacious room, with comfortable sofas and velvet side chairs arranged along the outer walls. I strained to see more of the room, raising up on my tippy toes to see above the heads of the crowd.

I spotted Stanton Collier's pewter coffin resting on its stand. Thank God it was a closed coffin. A large, framed portrait of him stood at the head of the casket. A massive, costly spray of white roses completely covered the coffin lid. His widow and daughter were both seated in the front row, legs crossed and hands folded primly in laps. I noticed they barely looked up as people filed past.

"Mrs. Collier ... Savannah, please accept my sincere condolences for your loss. This isn't the best time, but I wanted to thank you for your generous check that you sent to cover the wedding expenses at the inn."

Savannah stood and motioned me to follow her. We found a semi-private spot near a potted camellia plant in a corner.

"You're right, this isn't the place to discuss finances. Thank you for coming and offering your condolences, but you'll understand if my mother and I prefer to put your inn and any reminders of that wedding venue out of our minds. The entire thing has been a nightmare."

"I'm truly sorry you feel that way. I had hoped that when you and

Stephen were ready to take your vows that you'd return to Magnolia Blossom."

"Humph! If we ever get to that point of reconciliation, it would be a miracle. Frankly, I don't know where Stephen and I stand. I'm not sure our wedding will ever happen."

"That's too bad. You and Stephen seemed to love each other very much and I thought you made a beautiful couple. I guess your maid of honor is happy," I said and watched her reaction.

"What do you mean? Why would Susan be happy?" Savannah hissed.

"C'mon, you must have guessed how she felt about Stephen? You'd have to be blind not to see how Susan craved him. Now that you're out of the picture, she's got a clear path."

Savannah's shocked expression almost made me regret my words. I decided to press for answers while I had a chance. "Savannah, just how well do you know Susan? Where did the two of you meet?"

She shook her head, her eyes blank, as my words sunk in. "What? What did you ask me? I, um, met Susan at school. We were both at Emory & Henry University. She was in my sorority."

"So you didn't know her before school? Where is she from?"

"Why are you asking all these questions about Susan?"

"I'm just trying to learn as much information as I can about anyone who could have been involved with your father's death. Some other things have popped up too. If you have time, come back to the inn so we can talk," I offered. I touched her arm and pasted a sincere expression on my face, "I'm sorry to intrude on your sorrow. We'll leave now."

I stepped away from her and motioned to Lily and Lionel to follow me as we made our way back through the crowd toward the exit. Allen surprised me by clasping my elbow as I inched past a group of men. My eyes flashed to his as I felt the pressure of his hand on my arm. He led me out the door and stopped near a bench bordering a flower bed.

"What are you doing here?" We both asked at the same time.

"You go first," Allen said. He dropped his hand from my arm.

"Paying my respects to a client. Anything wrong with that? What are you doing?" I tossed the question back to him.

"Keeping an eye on potential suspects. Learn anything new?"

I glanced over at Lily and Lionel. Both were standing near, watching our ping-pong conversation. Raising an eyebrow and conveying a silent message to Lionel, I inclined my head and nodded toward a coffee shop across the street.

"How about a cup of coffee, detective?" asked Lionel. "I've got some interesting information I'd like to run by you."

Allen looked between us, weighing his decision, before agreeing. "All right. Let's get a coffee."

The four of us walked across the street to a local coffee shop and found a corner table that afforded us some privacy. After ordering coffee for all of us, we settled into an awkward silence as we each waited on the other to speak.

"Look, ever since that coin and hidden tunnel were found, I think it's fair to say that everything and everyone has been under suspicion. My nerves have been on edge living at the inn, especially knowing my home had literally been invaded. I've asked Lionel to help research people from that wedding party other than James Warner. Before you say anything, I know your chief wants to pin this mess on Sally. But I'm sure you'll agree with me she couldn't tie herself up in an underground tunnel," I said and stared straight at Allen.

"Agree. Sally isn't the likely murderer. That doesn't let her off as an accessory. I'm keeping my eye on James Warner and will arrest him for fraud and possible theft as soon as I can. I'm keeping an open mind as to him being the killer too," Allen said.

"Okay. I asked Lionel to dig into Susan Harper's past. I questioned Savannah today about her relationship with Susan. She just told me she met Susan while at Emory & Henry. They were sorority sisters."

Lionel leaned forward and lowered his voice as he shared his findings. "I made a deep dive into Susan Harper's identity—it didn't exist before her enrollment at Emory. No high school transcript, no employment records. I couldn't even find a birth certificate. Don't you find that strange?"

"I know you're good at your work, but you're sure?"

"Positive," Lionel stated without hesitation.

Allen leaned back in his chair as he considered this new development. "You think she changed her name? I've got her fingerprint sample, but the lab hasn't run them yet. They didn't put a priority on her because they were concentrated on the males."

"Hmm, that's rather a sexist attitude. Isn't it?" Lily asked with an unladylike snort.

"I suppose it is. What can I say? A bunch of Southern good ole boys run the lab. Women aren't supposed to be killers. But I guarantee you I'll put a rush on those prints today," Allen insisted. He drained his coffee cup then stood. He smiled at me before turning away. "I'll call you later."

I nodded and returned his smile. "I'll look forward to it, Yankee."

Chapter Thirteen

Allen

"Tom, I'm running into town to visit Sally at the hospital. When I'm done, I'll swing by the store and pick up those groceries plus the hardware supplies you wanted. Did you make me a list?" I asked him as I checked my cell phone for messages then tossed it into my purse.

"It's on the counter. Ask Joe at the hardware store for a bag of his eight-penny nails. I'll need them for closing that trap door shut."

"Okay, Tom. You got it. See y'all later."

I lucked out by finding a parking spot close to the hospital. A quick walk had me entering the lobby and taking the elevator to the third floor. The bell dinged as the doors slid open and I stepped out onto Sally's floor. Smells of disinfectant, strong cleaning detergents, and a few other scents I'd rather not know, assaulted my nose. Hospital aids pushed food carts down the hall and into patient rooms. Lunch time.

Rapping lightly on Sally's door, I didn't hear an answer. I carefully eased the door open in case she was asleep. Stopping cold, I glanced at the door to confirm I had the correct room number, then walked around the empty room. Where was she? Hurrying back to the nurses' station, I stood tapping my foot and waiting to gain the attention of the nurse on duty while she continued talking on the phone. Finally, she hung up and turned a polite smile on me.

"Yes? Can I help you?" the nurse inquired, glancing at the time on her watch.

"What happened to the patient in room twelve ... Sally Rawlins?"

The nurse picked up a clipboard, ran her finger down a list of names then raised her eyes. "She was discharged into the custody of the Charlottesville police. I believe they transported her."

"I see. Thank you," I said through a haze of anger.

I marched to the elevator and stepped into the first one, not caring whether it was going up or down when I punched the ground floor button. Sally is in custody ... well, we'll see about that. Operating on automation, I jumped into my truck and drove the short distance to the police station then parked along the curb. I didn't care if it was a short-term parking spot. Let them give me a ticket!

Storming into the Charlottesville station, my frustration simmered under the surface. It wasn't the first time I'd butted heads with Detective Allen Crawford, but this time felt different. This time, Sally was in jail, accused of murder. Sally—who, until recently, had been tied up in a basement, half-conscious, with no knowledge of the tunnel's existence. How could Allen believe she was capable of killing Stanton Collier?

I stepped through the heavy glass doors, the low hum of office noise —phones ringing, officers murmuring, and keyboards clacking greeted me. The familiar scent of coffee and a faint whiff of floor polish filled my nostrils as I made my way to the front desk.

"Detective Crawford," I said to the officer behind the counter, trying to keep my voice steady.

He gave me a nod, disappearing into the back office. A moment later, Allen emerged, looking weary and impatient, his brow furrowed. Dark circles appeared under his eyes, and his dark hair was messier than usual. He motioned me into one of the side rooms without a word. The heavy door shut behind us with a thud, and the sound echoed in the small, windowless room.

"Maddie, I'm not in the mood for another lecture," Allen said, sinking into the chair opposite me, rubbing a hand over his face. "We have procedures. Sally's being held for questioning—"

"She's *in jail* ," I snapped, leaning forward. "Not *being held,* Allen. You arrested her for a crime she didn't commit!"

"She was in the tunnel, Maddie. She admitted to helping Warner and his accomplice. The Chief says that makes her an accessory at the very least."

My pulse quickened. "Good gracious! She was kidnapped and held in that tunnel as a victim. That's not a reason to throw her in a cell. She's not capable of murder. You know that. You know she was coerced."

"Coerced or not, she's involved. My hands are tied."

I could feel my anger rising. "Involved? Or just a convenient scapegoat because you haven't figured out who really killed Collier?"

Allen's eyes darkened, and for a second, I thought I saw something beyond the stern detective facade—a flicker of pain, buried deep. His jaw clenched. "Don't do this, Maddie."

"Do what? Defend my friend? You've been riding this case so hard you're not even seeing what's in front of you. You're pushing me away when all I've done is try to help."

"That's the problem!" His voice raised an octave, sharp with frustration. He stood up and paced the small room. "You think you can just involve yourself in a murder investigation like it's some kind of puzzle or history exercise. This isn't a game. People are dead. Sally may not be the only one involved, but she knows more than she's telling us."

I froze. His words cut deeper than I expected. He'd never spoken to me like that before. It wasn't just about Sally—it was about me. Why was he pushing so hard? I narrowed my eyes, trying to understand the man in front of me. The one who had been so kind, and yet always kept me at arm's length when things got serious. Was I wrong about the feelings building between us?

"You're not just angry about the case," I said quietly, watching him stop in his tracks. "This is something else."

Allen's gaze shifted, avoiding mine for a moment, before he turned back toward me. The walls he kept up so meticulously cracked just a little, enough for me to glimpse the hurt he carried.

"There's nothing else. This is about the case."

"No, it's not." I stood up, walking toward him, trying to piece together what I sensed but didn't fully understand. I laid my hand on his shoulder, but he shrugged it away. "You push me away every time I get too close to figuring something out. You're overprotective, but at the same time, you keep shutting me out. Why?"

He let out a slow breath and sank back into the chair, his shoulders slumping. He stared at his hands for a moment before finally meeting my eyes. His voice softened, the usual bravado replaced by something more raw.

"There was someone ... back in Philly." His voice was strained, like he was dragging the words from a place he didn't want to go. "Her name was Olivia. We were close ... together for years. She was everything to me."

I didn't breathe. I didn't blink. The way his voice wavered, the pain that flickered across his features—it was like he'd just opened a door he'd sworn to keep locked forever.

"During a robbery," he continued, his voice lower now, "I responded to a call. She was at the wrong place, at the wrong time. Got caught in the crossfire. And I couldn't ... I couldn't save her."

The room felt colder suddenly, the walls closing in. My heart ached for him, for the burden he carried. I finally understood why he acted the way he did—why he kept me at arm's length. Why he was so protective, but always held back.

"That's why," he said, his jaw tightening again, "I don't want you involved, Maddie. I can't go through that again. I don't want to lose someone else that I care for."

I didn't know what to say. My anger dissolved into something else, something more complicated. He cared for me. He just admitted it. I could feel the tension between us, the push and pull of emotions we'd both been avoiding. But this wasn't just about me anymore—this was about Sally. And Stanton Collier. And finding the truth.

"I'm sorry," I said softly, taking a step closer. "I didn't know."

He looked away, his hand running through his hair. "I know you want to help, but this is dangerous, Maddie. Sally might be in over her head, but I still think she's hiding something."

"What about the footprints in the basement? The ones leading toward the chest?" I asked. "They weren't Sally's, were they?"

He hesitated before answering. "No. They don't match hers."

"Think Allen, the gold coin in the trunk—Sally didn't have access to the trunk, right? Lionel found the buried key. No one else could have opened that trunk. We had difficulty unlocking it."

Allen sighed, rubbing his temples. "No, but ..."

I could see the conflict in his eyes. He wasn't ready to let Sally off the hook, but he knew there were more pieces to the puzzle.

"What if she's just a pawn in this? What if James Warner and someone else—maybe Susan Harper—are the real players?" I suggested, hoping to break through his stubbornness. "There's more going on than we realize, Allen. The gold coin, the tunnels, the treasure, the murder ... they're all connected."

"I know." He shook his head. "But I can't ignore what we've got so far. Sally confessed to helping unlock doors and getting them tools."

"She was coerced!" I exclaimed. "You heard her—she didn't know what she was getting into. And for her help, all the thanks she got was to be blindfolded and thrown into a cellar. Allen, she's a scared victim, not a killer."

He stood up again, running a hand through his hair in frustration.

"I don't know what to believe anymore. Every lead feels like it's slipping through my fingers."

I reached out, touching his arm gently. "Then let's figure it out together. Stop pushing me away. We're better off working together than at odds."

For a moment, he didn't respond. But then his expression softened, and he nodded slowly. "Alright. But you have to promise me—if things get dangerous, you'll step back. No more risking your life, Maddie." His fingers lightly caressed the side of my face.

"I'll be careful," I said, giving him a reassuring smile. "But we both know I'm not stepping back."

He rolled his eyes but didn't argue. "Fine. Let's go back over everything and figure out what we're missing."

The room felt lighter somehow, the tension between us shifting into something more comfortable. We weren't done arguing, I knew that much—but at least now we understood each other a little better. And maybe, just maybe, we'd be able to solve this mystery together.

As I stood to leave, my phone buzzed in my pocket. It was Lionel. I put him on speakerphone.

"Where are you? I've got a lead on Susan Harper."

I glanced at Allen, my heart racing again. "Looks like we've got work to do."

"Let's go meet your friend then," Allen said as he slipped his gun in his holster and tossed his suit coat over his shoulder.

Chapter Fourteen

Susan

Driving past the university campus, I followed Allen's sedan on our way to meet Lionel at his office in the African-American Heritage Center. We both pulled into the parking lot a few minutes later. Lionel met us in the lobby and ushered us back to his private office. I waved a hello to Lee Warner as I walked past his open door.

"Hello Maddie." Lee looked up and acknowledged me as I passed.

"C'mon in," Lionel said as we took seats around a small conference table strewn with computer print-outs.

"Okay, so what did you find that we had to hurry over to hear?" I asked him.

Lionel grinned, clearly proud of his investigative skills. "I found out Susan Harper's real last name."

"Harding." Lionel and Allen both announced the name at the same time.

Poor Lionel, his big surprise deflated like a flat balloon.

"How did you ...?

"Ran her prints. Just got the report back this morning."

"So her last name is really Harding. Where does that get us?" I asked the two men sitting next to me.

"Susan Harding is from Durham, North Carolina. We found some misdemeanor charges listed on her for petty shoplifting," Allen said.

"I learned her father's name was Earl Harding. His obituary was posted in the Durham Herald, that's where I saw Susan included with his heirs. I've been wracking my brain trying to recall where I know the name Earl Harding from. It'll come to me. It feels important too, so frustrating, but I'll think of it. I'll keep digging for more information on him. Once I concentrate on something else, it will pop into my mind where I know him," Lionel said.

"You let me know when you do, okay?" Allen asked Lionel.

"Ditto. Keep me informed. Well, fellas, if that's all for now, I've got shopping to do. See you later," I said as I pushed my chair back and moved to the door. "Thanks Lionel, for working on this."

"Sure. No problem. Now if we can just figure out where the rest of that gold treasure is, I'd be really happy."

"Yes sir, you and me both," I said with a chuckle and a backward wave over my shoulder as I headed down the hall and out the door.

Main Street in Clarkstown bustled with afternoon shoppers and townsfolk going about their business. Small shops, one bank, Dora's café, and two gas stations comprised the bulk of the town's business district. Basically, we were a small rural community that depended on our agriculture and whatever tourist dollars we could siphon off the overflow from Charlottesville to build our economy.

Vehicles crammed into the parking lot at the Piggly-Wiggly grocery store in Clarkstown. I was lucky to squeeze my pickup into a narrow space. *The store must be promoting a BOGO – buy one get one sale,* I thought, as I walked toward the entrance. Grabbing a buggy, I checked my list and started down the first aisle. My eyes scanned the shelves, searching for the brand Tom preferred for canned corn, beets, and okra.

I'd have to swing by the farmer's market later for the fresh green beans and asparagus to add to our larder.

Hmm, what's next on the list? I pushed my buggy slowly down the aisle, reading my notes. Concentrating on what Tom needed and not watching where I was going. Too late, I bumped into another shopper's cart. I glanced up and recognized Mrs. Ginther. Oh no! Good gracious, the biggest gossip in town just smiled like the cat who had caught the canary.

"Hello Madison! Out shopping today? My goodness, you've certainly been busy at the inn. You look all right though; I thought you'd appear all frazzled. I hear the police have been there every day this week," Mrs. Ginther exclaimed in a voice that half the store could hear.

"How are you today, Mrs. Ginther? Please tell me you aren't believing all those silly rumors about the Magnolia Blossom Inn."

"What rumors, dear?"

I took a deep breath. I had put my foot in it now with the opening she needed to quiz me further. Smiling sweetly, I tried to steer the conversation to safer topics.

"The inn is hosting weddings now. I've completely renovated the barn into a banquet hall. You'll have to see it when you come out to pick apples this month. Our Lodi apples are ready now and I believe those sweet ginger golds might ripen early this year. Y'all be sure to come out."

Maneuvering around the end of her buggy, I hurried away from her, leaving the woman staring at me with her mouth open. Whew! That was a close call. I'll have to check each aisle to make sure I don't encounter her again while I shopped.

My cart filled up quickly with jars of peanut butter and an assortment of jam, several jars of applesauce, cans of peaches, and a couple boxes of cake mixes. Having so many guests staying for both breakfast and suppers had really depleted our pantry. Now I only needed to add two boxes of laundry detergent and some dishwasher soap, plus more paper towels to complete my order. Shoppers crowded the store, but I paused to survey each section before I ventured forth lest I get trapped by my gossip-loving friend. Checking to assure it was safe, I made my way to the checkout stands.

One of Grannie's dearest friends, Mrs. Amanda Fitzwilliams, waited for the cashier to count out her change. She was a sweet elderly woman, with silver hair wearing that bluish rinse women her age seemed to get. Amanda had taught elementary school for over forty years. She knew everyone in Clarkstown and likely had taught both the parents and their children in her classroom over the years. Seeing her, I pushed my buggy in line behind her. She turned and smiled broadly when she recognized me.

"Hello, Maddie dear. How are you getting on in that big empty house? Oh, I do so miss your grandmother. Sunday bridge isn't the same without her."

"Hello Miss Amanda. I'm doing just fine, thank you. I hope y'all been feeling well. Without guests at the inn, it does get pretty quiet. Please stop by for an afternoon tea sometime. I'd love to visit with you."

"That's kind of you to offer, dear. I do hope that nonsense that I've heard about a lost Confederate treasure isn't true. My goodness, I wonder what Polly would have thought about that."

Our conversation had drawn unwelcome listeners from surrounding shoppers. "I'm sure she would have agreed with you, that it's all nonsense. Nothing like that exists," I said, hoping to dissuade any potential treasure hunters in the store. The last thing I needed were more people trying to strike it rich by digging up our farm.

After loading grocery sacks onto the front passenger seat and floorboard of the pickup, I headed out for the next stop. The hardware store was a short distance in the next block. I parked a few doors away and strolled into the shady storefront. Handmade straw brooms stood just inside the doorway. A large open barrel held bundles of kindling. The scent of freshly hewn lumber hung in the air. Wiley's Hardware prided itself on being a one-stop shop for the do-it-yourselfer, or professional home repairer. Plumbing supplies, electrical outlets and wiring, hand tools, gardening seeds and bulbs, plus every possible variety of hardware fasteners filled the organized shop.

Joe Wiley stood behind the counter reading a copy of the Gazette sports page. He nodded as I entered.

"What can I do for you today, Miss Maddie? Tom send you?"

"Yes, he did Joe. Can I get a pound of your eight-penny nails? Tom has a construction project he's working on."

"Sure thing. Just give me a minute," the owner said as he strolled toward the back of the store, where bins of loose nails, screws, washers, bolts, and nuts of varying sizes filled the aisle.

I glanced at the newspaper headlines while I waited. My mind drifted to the endless to-do list waiting for me back at the inn. The old farmhouse was charming, but it needed constant upkeep, and today's mission was to pick up supplies that Tom needed to finish nailing shut that cellar door. I wouldn't sleep well until I knew that passage no longer existed.

"Here you go. This ought to hold him unless ole Tom's fixin' to build a new wing onto that house," Joe said with a laugh.

"Thanks. What do I owe you?" I asked.

"About three-fifty, I'll just put it on your tab. No worries. Give Tom my best," Joe said as he handed me the paper sack filled with nails.

"You have a good day." I smiled at him and walked toward the door. That's when I heard a familiar voice.

Someone was talking low; the voice sounded familiar but also off—like the person was trying hard to sound different. I stood in the hardware doorway and scanned the immediate space. Next door, hidden by the barber shop's recessed entrance, stood Susan Harper. A phone pressed to her ear, she had her back turned to any pedestrians.

There was something strange about her posture, stiff and rigid. Her voice, though, was what caught my attention the most. It was deep, almost ... masculine? Like she purposefully lowered it to sound threatening. I remembered Sally describing a masculine voice in the tunnel. Was that it? My curiosity piqued. I ducked behind the stack of hay bales near the hardware store's entrance, trying to catch more of her conversation.

"I don't care what you think," Susan said, her voice clipped and controlled. "We need to find those coins. And fast. The longer we wait, the more people will start poking around. I'm not leaving without them."

Coins? My stomach flipped. Was she talking about the gold?

I crouched a little lower behind the bales, the bag of nails rattled as I shifted it in my hands. She was talking fast now, giving orders, as though she were the one in charge of some larger plan.

"I'll meet you later," Susan said firmly, her tone sharp. "No excuses this time. Yeah, that's right. Don't screw this up."

The call ended, and I froze as she turned in my direction, scanning the street with narrowed eyes. I ducked lower, heart pounding against my rib cage.

Susan slipped her phone into her pocket and began walking briskly, her sandals slapping against the sidewalk. I hesitated for just a moment before deciding to follow her.

I trailed behind her, keeping a safe distance, darting into doorways and behind cars whenever she glanced back. She moved quickly, cutting through side streets and alleys, her pace picked up as she neared the edge of town and away from people.

Where was she headed? I debated with myself whether I should phone Allen now or keep following her until I knew her destination.

Susan made the decision for me. I had lost sight of her for barely a minute when I felt a gun barrel poking me in the back with her voice hissing in my ear.

"Playing detective again, Maddie? I knew you were behind me so I led you away from town. Stupid fool. You played right into my hands.You're coming with me now. I want to introduce you to my twin brother, Carl. We want to know all about that gold you found in your basement."

Chapter Fifteen

Kidnapped

I should have listened to that gnawing feeling in my gut, the one that told me something wasn't right the moment I spotted Susan Harper outside the store. It wasn't just her voice—low and ominous, almost masculine as she hissed orders into her phone. It was the way she moved, like she didn't belong there; as if she was trying to slip away unnoticed. Now, here I was, paying the price for not trusting my instincts.

My heart raced as I stared at Susan, her eyes cold and calculating, standing in the doorway of the abandoned cabin. She had led me through town like a ghost, too quick and too careful to be caught, until I foolishly followed and allowed myself to be trapped. My hands tied together in front of me, I sat on the floor in this rundown place at the edge of the woods. Carl—her hulking, brutish brother—hovered over me, pacing nervously while she barked orders at him. He grunted in reply.

"You should've stayed out of this, Maddie," Susan said, her voice icy as she leaned against the wall. "I had everything under control until you decided to play Nancy Drew."

"I wasn't trying to—" I started, my voice shaking, but Susan cut me off with a sharp laugh.

"Don't lie to me," she snapped, her eyes narrowing. "You've been snooping around since the day that crook Stanton Collier died. You and your friends."

Carl, standing by the window, flinched at her words. His eyes darted from me to his twin sister, and I could see the anxiety rolling off him in waves. He wasn't as calm as Susan. He was jittery, hands trembling slightly as they fidgeted with the hem of his shirt. He wasn't built for this. Susan was the mastermind, and Carl was her puppet, too afraid to defy her.

I swallowed hard, my throat dry. "Look, Susan, I don't know what you think I know, but I'm not after your treasure or whatever it is you're looking for. I was just out grocery shopping, and—"

"Shopping?" Susan scoffed, taking a step closer to me. She crossed her arms, glaring down at me like a predator. "Do you really expect me to believe that? You've been sticking your nose in places it doesn't belong. I know you've been in the tunnels. I know you found the gold coin. Don't play dumb with me."

I opened my mouth to protest, but the truth was, I had found the coin. And I had been in the tunnels. But Susan didn't know Allen and I had sealed that passage. Still, I didn't know more about the gold Susan was after—at least, not all of it. I wasn't even sure there was a treasure beyond that one coin.

"Susan, please," I said, keeping my voice calm, hoping to buy time. "I swear, I don't know anything about the treasure. I'm just trying to run the inn, keep things together. I never meant to get involved in all this."

"Oh, I'm sure you didn't mean to," Susan said, her tone dripping with sarcasm. "But now you're involved whether you like it or not. And unless you want to end up like Collier, you're going to tell me everything you know about the gold and where it's hidden."

I felt my stomach drop at her words. End up like Collier. She had no problem admitting it now—Susan had killed him. She was dangerous, and I had to tread carefully. I could feel the ropes biting into my wrists as I shifted, trying to loosen them without drawing attention to myself.

Carl's pacing grew more frantic, and he glanced at me, his eyes wide with fear. "Susan, we don't need to do this. She doesn't know anything. I didn't plan on murder. Let's just leave."

I listened closely to his voice. No southern twang, his words carried more of a mid-west or northern accent. Was it Carl that Sally had heard in the tunnel?

Susan whirled on him, her voice sharp as a whip. "Shut up, Carl. We're not leaving without that gold. It's ours, payment for Collier ruining Dad. Whatever it takes, I'm not walking away now."

Carl flinched at her words, but he didn't argue. He just kept pacing, his shoulders hunched like he was trying to make himself smaller. I could see the fear in his eyes—the fear of Susan, the fear of getting caught. He wasn't a killer. He was scared; trapped just like I was.

I had to get out of here. But how? I glanced around the cabin, my mind racing. Planks covered the windows and Susan blocked the only door. There was no easy way out. My pulse pounded in my ears as I struggled to stay calm. I directed my questions to Carl.

"You carried Sally into the tunnel, didn't you? Why? Did you think she knew about the treasure chest? Sally is a mere housekeeper at the inn; she's only worked there six months. I know she helped James Warner but did she help you too?"

Susan answered me as she shook her head at Carl, "Yeah, we put her in the tunnel. She's another one that snooped where she didn't belong. James bragged to her about the gold and she thought he'd share it. The silly chit fell for it. That con artist didn't have a clue where the treasure was. But you do."

"No, you're wrong. I don't have the treasure," I said, my voice steady despite the fear gnawing at my insides. "I swear. I only found one coin. Whatever you're looking for—it's not at the inn."

Susan's eyes flickered with something—doubt, maybe, or frustration—but she didn't soften. She leaned in closer, her voice a low hiss. "You're lying. I know you are. I've been planning for months to get even with Stanton Collier. Savannah gave me the perfect opportunity. That Confederate gold was going to be the icing on the cake. It's got to be there and I want it. Why else would your family have kept that old trunk for all these years?"

"You knew about the trunk? Why didn't you open it? Guess you didn't find the key, is that it?" I taunted her.

"Where's that key now?" Susan demanded.

I swallowed hard, trying to hold her gaze, but my heart was racing. Did my grandfather know about the treasure? Could it be true? I had a hard time believing that. Wouldn't Grannie have said so?

Suddenly, my phone buzzed in my pocket. I tensed, praying they wouldn't hear it, but Carl's eyes shot to my jeans.

"She's got a phone!" he yelped, stepping forward as if he had finally found something to do. "Susan, she's got a phone. She could have called someone."

Susan's eyes blazed with fury, and she marched over, ripping the phone from my pocket. She glanced at the screen; her face twisting in anger. "It's Detective Crawford," she snarled. "Looks like your knight in shining armor is worried about you, Maddie."

She threw the phone onto the floor, and it shattered with a sharp crack. "Too bad he won't find you in time."

My heart sank. Allen. He had to know something was wrong, but would he be able to find me? And even if he did, would it be too late?

Susan grabbed my arm, yanking me to my feet. "You're coming with us. We're going to the inn, and you're going to show us exactly where the treasure is."

"I don't know where it is!" I protested, panic rising in my chest.

"Shut up!" Susan hissed. "We'll find it, one way or another. You're just going to help speed things up."

Carl's face had gone pale. He looked like he might be sick. "Susan, this is getting out of hand. We should leave."

"We're not leaving without the gold!" Susan shouted, turning on him. "Stop being such a coward, Carl! We're so close. Don't ruin this now."

I could see Carl's resolve crumbling, but he didn't argue. He just stood there, staring at the floor, while Susan tightened her grip on my arm.

I had to think fast. I couldn't let them take me to the inn. If they did, I'd be putting everyone in danger—Tom, Lionel, even Allen. And I wasn't about to let them tear apart my home searching for treasure that might not even exist.

"Susan, wait," I said, trying to stall, trying to come up with a plan. "There's something else—something you don't know."

Susan's eyes narrowed. "What are you talking about?"

"I—I heard Stanton talking to James Warner about the treasure before he died," I lied, hoping it would buy me some time. "He said something about another piece of the puzzle, something hidden outside the inn. I think I might know where it is."

Susan stared at me, her eyes searching mine for any sign of deceit. I held my breath, praying she'd take the bait.

"Where?" she demanded.

I swallowed hard. "In the orchard, near the old stone well. It's buried there. Stanton said it was the key to finding the rest of the treasure. That must be why James asked Sally to unlock the shed; he needed a shovel."

Susan glanced at Carl, then back at me. For a moment, I thought she might believe me.

But then her lips curled into a cruel smile. "Nice try, Maddie. But I'm not falling for that."

Before I could react, she shoved me hard, and I stumbled backward, hitting the ground with a thud. Pain shot through my shoulder as I landed awkwardly, but I didn't have time to dwell on it.

Susan stood over me, her face twisted in anger. "You're not as clever as you think. But don't worry—we'll find the gold. And when we do, you'll wish you'd never gotten involved."

I struggled to sit up, my mind racing. I had to find a way out of this. But how?

Meanwhile, Allen drove up and down the streets of Clarkstown with Tom Borden riding next to him scanning for signs of Maddie's Ram pickup. As they left the market parking lot and headed down the side street, Tom pointed.

"There! Stop! That's her truck."

Both men jumped out of the police cruiser and ran to the parked vehicle. Allen and Tom stood beside the aged pickup truck, their faces grim, as they looked through the windows. The groceries Maddie had bought earlier were still stacked on the floor and seat, untouched.

"She never made it home," Tom said quietly, his voice filled with worry. "She was supposed to buy a bag of nails at the hardware store too. Maybe Joe can tell us something."

Allen and Tom entered the Wiley Hardware store and found Joe at his usual spot behind the counter, working a crossword puzzle. He looked up as they approached.

"Hey Tom, what's up?"

Allen spoke first. "Was Maddie Brooke in here earlier today?"

Joe glanced between the two men. A frown wrinkled his brow. "Yes sir, she was here. What's wrong?"

"What time did you see Maddie?" asked Tom. He shifted back and forth, rocking on the balls of his feet.

"Hmm, dunno exactly. Wait a second. I recorded her purchase on this here new accounting system my boy set up. Lemme see now, yep, here it is ... two-forty-five."

"Thanks. Did you see anyone around when she left? Did she speak with anyone?" Allen asked.

"Sorry, no. Can't say that I did. I was in the back helping a customer after Maddie left."

"Okay."

Allen and Tom stepped outside and stood on the sidewalk, scanning the street.

"I'm glad you called me. You did the right thing." Allen's jaw clenched as he scanned the area, his heart pounding with fear and frustration. "She's in trouble," he muttered. "I can feel it."

Tom nodded, his expression tense. "We need to find her. Now. I bet it's that crazy family from the wedding. Strange things have happened ever since they arrived at the inn."

Allen's eyes narrowed as he considered the possibilities. Maddie wouldn't have just disappeared. Something had happened, and it wasn't good.

"You know this area better than me. Where could someone hide? Can you think of any vacant houses, caves, somewhere a person could hide?"

Tom scratched his head. "Let me think a minute."

Chapter Sixteen

Trapped

I hadn't meant to stumble into the truth—at least not this way. It was like piecing together a complicated puzzle, each fragment clicking into place with growing dread. The false name, the hidden vendetta motive, the secret passage—it all fit now, and the final piece was Susan. But now, as I sat in the dark, musty cabin, my heart pounding against my ribcage, I realized the truth was far more dangerous than I had ever imagined.

Susan wasn't just a disgruntled friend of the bride in love with the groom. She was Susan Harding, and she had more at stake than a ruined wedding or lost treasure. She had revenge on her mind.

The air in the cabin was thick, the only light seeped in through cracks in the wood-covered windows. Susan stood across from me, her eyes cold and calculating.

I swallowed hard, trying to steady my nerves. My voice shook slightly, but I forced myself to stay calm. "Susan, or should I say, Susan Harding ... I know you killed Stanton. What did he have to do with your father?"

Her lips curled into a smirk, but there was no humor in her eyes—only fury, barely contained. "Of course you do. You've been playing detective since the start, haven't you? Poking your nose into things that don't concern you."

"You made it my concern when you committed murder at my inn."

I glanced toward the door, calculating my chances of making a run for it. Slim to none. I was cornered in this remote cabin, deep in the woods outside Clarkstown. Even if I made it out, Carl was probably lurking nearby, just waiting for an excuse to drag me back.

"Why, Susan? Why kill him?" I asked, my voice cracking as I tried to keep her talking. Maybe if I could get her to see reason. "This revenge— it won't fix anything. It won't bring him back."

Susan's eyes darkened, and she took a step toward me, her fists clenched. Her voice took on a deep masculine tone as she growled, "You don't get it, do you? You can't possibly understand what he did to my family. Stanton Collier stole the patent of my father's invention for microchips used in hospital ultrasound machines. We would have been rich. Instead, Collier destroyed my father—ruined his business and left him with nothing. Nothing! We lost everything. And you want to stand there and tell me that revenge won't fix things?"

Her voice had risen to a fever pitch, and I felt a chill run down my spine. "I'm sorry for what happened to your father," I said softly, choosing my words carefully. "But Stanton's death won't undo the past. It's only going to destroy more lives—yours, your brother's. You're not murderers, Susan."

Susan let out a sharp laugh, the sound hollow and bitter. "Aren't we? Do you think we had a choice?" She paced the small room, the floor-boards creaking beneath her feet. "My father didn't have a choice when Stanton Collier stole everything from him. And when he ... when he took his own life. Carl and I didn't have a choice either. We had to do something."

She glared at me as she continued her rant. "I swallowed my pride and sweet-talked that simpering southern belle, Savannah —pretending to be her friend. Joining that sniveling bunch of girls in the sorority, I plotted to get close to her. Then when she asked me to be part of her wedding, I knew I finally had my chance. I must say, it was considerate of you to provide a loaded weapon readily available. I wasn't expecting that kind of hospitality from the inn."

Her voice wavered for a moment, and I saw a flicker of vulnerability, just a hint of the pain she had buried beneath her rage. But it was fleeting. She gave a short laugh. Her expression hardened again, and she looked at me with an icy glare.

"I'm not going to let you ruin this, Maddie. You've been a thorn in my side from the moment you got involved. But it ends here. As soon as it gets dark, you're going to show me where you hid that gold."

My heart hammered in my chest. She wasn't going to let me leave.

"Please, Susan," I said, my voice trembling despite my efforts to stay calm. "You don't have to do this. It's not too late to stop."

But she wasn't listening. Her focus shifted to the door as it creaked open, revealing a shadowed figure—Carl. His broad, hulking form filled the doorway, and my stomach lurched with fear. He stepped inside, his expression twisted with panic.

"Susan," he said, his voice low and urgent. "We've got a problem."

Susan turned to him, her brow furrowing. "What now?"

"It's the cop—Crawford," Carl muttered, glancing at me with a sneer. "He's snooping around town and heading this way."

My breath caught. Allen was getting closer.

"Did he see you?" Susan demanded, her voice sharp.

Carl shook his head. "No. We need to move—now."

Susan cursed under her breath, her gaze flicking to me. "This is your fault, Maddie. You've been too nosy for your own good."

Carl shifted nervously by the door, his eyes darting between me and his sister. I could see the tension in his posture, the nervous energy that radiated off him. He wasn't the one in control here—Susan was.

"Just let me go," I pleaded, trying to keep my voice steady. "You can still get out of this. It's not too late."

Susan's expression hardened, and she took a step toward me, her jaw clenched. "Do you think I'm stupid, Maddie? If I let you go, you'll tell everyone what you've figured out. You'll ruin everything and I won't get my gold."

Carl shuffled his feet, clearly uncomfortable with the situation. "Susan, maybe we should—"

"Shut up, Carl," she snapped, her eyes flashing with anger. "I know what I'm doing."

But Carl didn't look so sure. His gaze flickered toward me for a moment, and I could see the uncertainty in his eyes. Maybe I wasn't the only one who thought this plan was spiraling out of control.

I had to keep talking, had to keep them distracted until Allen found me or I could escape.

"Your father wouldn't want this," I said, my voice shaking. "He wouldn't want you to throw your lives away like this. Killing Stanton was wrong, and you know it."

Susan's lips curled into a bitter smile. "You didn't know my father. He was a genius and deserved justice for Collier's theft of his ideas. My father's company went bankrupt. He lost everything he had worked for his entire life. Ultimately, it killed him. My father didn't pull that trigger ... Stanton Collier did as sure as if his hand was on the gun. Well now Earl Harding is finally getting his justice."

I swallowed hard, my throat dry. "Revenge isn't justice, Susan. It's just more pain. Look at what it's done to you, to Carl. You're better than this."

Susan's expression faltered for just a second, and I saw a flicker of doubt in her eyes. But then she shook her head as if shaking off my words. "No, Maddie. It's too late for that."

Carl shifted uncomfortably by the door, his face pale. "Maybe she's right, Susan. Maybe we should—"

"Quiet, Carl!" Susan snapped, her voice cutting through the tension like a knife. She turned back to me, her eyes blazing with fury. "We're too far in to turn back now. This ends here."

My heart raced, and I glanced toward the door, hoping for any sign of Allen. But there was nothing—just the looming threat of Susan and her brother.

"Please," I whispered, my voice trembling. "Don't do this."

Susan aimed her revolver straight at me.

Lionel spread the map out across his desktop. He put his cell phone on speaker as he compared the coordinates with the map and spoke to the anxious detective on the other end of the line.

"I remembered where I heard the name Earl Harding. He invented the first microchip used by ultra-sound machines. His name is on the patent but somewhere along the line Stanton Collier's name is credited for it. Harding was a big man in the tech world," Lionel said as he worked. "Okay, mark down these GPS coordinates. I've got a fix on Maddie."

"Are you sure, Lionel? Double-check those figures again please. We've got to find Maddie. My gut tells me Susan Harding has her. Susan's already killed once, she won't hesitate to do it again."

"Good thing Maddie allowed me to turn on the app for location tracking the last time she lost her phone. We should be able to track her location. Let's just hope she's in the same place as her phone," Lionel said in a soft voice as worry clouded his thoughts.

Lionel read the geo-tracking numbers to Allen then ran his finger across the road map as he found the geographic location.

"Thanks buddy. I'm on my way there now."

Chapter Seventeen

Safe

Holding my breath, I waited for the click of the revolver and the bullet that would end my life. In that split second, I swear my life flashed before my eyes—Grannie's ghost offering unsolicited advice, lazy afternoons at the Magnolia Blossom Inn, Luke curled up by the fire, and even Allen, frustrating as he could be. To my surprise, Carl leaped on his sister and knocked the gun out of her hand. It skidded across the floor, coming to rest against the far wall.

"Carl, you idiot!" Susan shrieked, her face twisting in rage as she tried to shove him off her.

"I can't do this anymore, Susan! We're in too deep!" Carl's voice cracked, his body trembling as he wrestled with her, his strength clearly no match for the force of her anger.

It was all the opportunity I needed.

I jumped to my feet and dashed out the open cabin door. Sprinting as fast as my feet could carry me, I ran for the cover of the dense forest. The thick, humid air engulfed my lungs as I ran. Rope bit into my tied hands and my side ached with each step, but I kept going, adrenaline surging through my veins. Plunging forward, trying to keep my balance, I ducked under low branches and pushed through thick underbrush. I was desperate to put as much distance between myself and the cabin as possible.

Just keep running, I told myself. *Don't look back.*

A shot rang out behind me. The sharp crack of a bullet hit the bark of a nearby tree, sending a fresh wave of panic coursing through me. Too close. Way too close.

My legs screamed in protest, my lungs on fire, but I forced myself to run faster, dodging around trees and leaping over exposed roots. The woods felt endless. My sense of direction spun upside down. I just needed to get away.

The sound of footsteps crashing through the underbrush behind me sent my heart into overdrive. They were coming after me. I didn't dare look back to see who it was—Susan, Carl, maybe both of them—I didn't know, but I could hear them getting closer with each passing second.

I stumbled, nearly tripping over a gnarled root hidden beneath the leaves, and my breath hitched in my throat. I couldn't afford to fall. Not now. Not when I was so close to—*To what?* I had no idea. I could be running straight toward my captors, for all I knew.

As I pushed through a particularly thick patch of brambles, my shirt caught on a thorny branch, slowing me down. I ripped it free, leaving a scrap of fabric hanging on the branch. The delay was enough for me to hear Susan's voice in the distance, cold and commanding.

"Find her, Carl! She can't have gone far!"

I paused for a moment, frantically searching for a hiding place. There was no way I could outrun them much longer. My rubbery legs felt like they might give out at any moment. My heart hammered in my chest. I glanced around, spotting a cluster of large rocks to my left, half-hidden by a fallen tree.

There. That'll have to do.

I slipped behind the rocks, crouching low and trying to control my ragged breathing. My heart pounded in my ears, making it almost impossible to hear anything else. Bending my head, I wiped sweat from my brow on my shirt and peeked through a small gap between the rocks.

Carl and Susan were arguing again, their voices growing louder as they approached.

"This is all your fault, Carl!" Susan snarled, her face flushed with fury. "You had one job—to keep her from getting away. And now look at us!"

"I never wanted to hurt her," Carl mumbled, his eyes darting nervously around the woods, as if expecting me to leap out at any moment. "She's not like Collier, Susan. She's just a girl, running that inn. I didn't sign up for this."

"Don't be stupid," Susan snapped. "She knows too much. We can't leave any loose ends."

My stomach twisted at her words. 'Loose ends.' That's all I was to her—a problem to be erased.

I held my breath, praying they wouldn't find me. My hiding spot was far from perfect, but with any luck, they'd pass right by without noticing.

Suddenly, Carl stopped dead in his tracks. "Did you hear that?"

My blood froze. Had they heard me?

"I didn't hear anything," Susan growled, but she was on high alert now, scanning the area with narrowed eyes. She gripped the gun tightly in her hand, her knuckles white.

"I think she went this way," Carl muttered, pointing to a patch of dense foliage just beyond my hiding place.

Susan followed his gaze, her expression dark and determined. "Let's go."

As they moved off in the opposite direction, I allowed myself a silent sigh of relief. But I knew it wouldn't last long. They were still hunting me. It was only a matter of time before they realized I'd doubled back or they found a way to trap me again.

I needed to get to Allen. I trusted him to come looking for me—he had to be nearby. He wasn't the kind to sit idly by when something felt off. If I could just get a signal out to him or somehow leave a clue, maybe—just maybe—I could get out of this alive.

Slowly, I crept out from behind the rocks, careful to stay as low and silent as possible. My legs trembled from the exertion, and I knew I couldn't run much farther. I just had to be smart. I had to stay hidden, stay quiet, and find a way to reach Allen.

I heard a rustling in the distance, and my heart leaped into my throat. But this noise sounded different—lighter, more deliberate.

"Madison!" The voice was a hoarse whisper, but I knew it instantly.

Allen. Thank God.

I turned, spotting him just beyond the trees, crouching low and moving with the kind of precision that only a seasoned cop could manage. Relief flooded my chest, and for a brief moment, I felt like I could breathe again.

I tried to get his attention without making too much noise. Allen's eyes locked onto mine, and I could see the flash of recognition on his face. He darted toward me, his expression a mixture of relief and determination.

"Maddie! Are you okay?" he whispered, his voice low but urgent. He pulled a knife off his belt and cut my ropes, freeing my hands.

"I'm better now that you're here," I breathed, rubbing my hands and wrists to restore my circulation. I clutched his arm. "But Susan and her brother—they're still out here."

"Who? Did you say brother?"

"Yes."

Allen's jaw tightened, and he glanced around, his hand resting on his holstered gun. "I figured Susan was our killer but I didn't know she had a brother; thought it was Warner working with her. We've got backup on the way. Stay close to me, and don't make a sound."

Before I could respond, the crunch of footsteps echoed behind us. Carl's voice drifted through the trees, panicked and breathless.

"Susan! I think I saw something! Over here!"

Allen's eyes flicked toward the noise, and without missing a beat, he grabbed my hand, pulling me into the shadows. We crouched low, our breaths shallow as Carl and Susan's footsteps grew louder, closer.

They were nearly on top of us now, so close I could see Carl's anxious face through the gaps in the leaves. Susan trailed behind him, her gun still in hand, her expression twisted with frustration.

"We have to move," Allen whispered in my ear, his breath warm against my skin. "Now."

Before I could fully process what was happening, Allen tugged me forward, guiding me deeper into the woods. We moved quickly but quietly, each step measured and careful. I didn't dare look back.

Suddenly, Susan's voice rang out again, sharp and furious. "Carl! I swear if you don't find her, I'll—"

But I didn't hear the rest. Allen had already pulled me further into the cover of the trees, and with each step ... the cabin and my captors grew more distant.

We didn't stop until we reached a clearing where Tom and two other officers stood waiting, their eyes wide with concern.

"Maddie!" Tom rushed toward me, his face etched with worry. "Thank God, you're okay."

I nodded weakly, my legs trembling beneath me. "I—I thought I wasn't going to make it."

Allen gave my hand a reassuring squeeze. "You're safe now."

Glancing back toward the woods, I knew I wouldn't be totally safe until the police caught Susan Harding and her brother.

Officers spread out and began combing the forest in search of Susan and Carl Harding. Tom stayed close, fretting like a dowager aunt, while Allen kept me within the circle of his embrace. I tried to speak but my teeth chattered and my voice caught in my throat.

"It's all right. You're experiencing some shock. Take a couple deep breaths. You'll be fine. I've got you now and I'm not letting go," Allen said as he pulled me closer against his solid chest and pressed a kiss to the top of my head.

I sighed and snuggled closer, feeling the heat from his body, finally, I began to relax.

"How did you know where to search?" I was finally able to ask him.

"Lionel. Your phone has a GPS tracking app."

I chuckled, so grateful for my wonderful tech wizard friend.

"Of course. I should have known. Lionel insisted on installing that location service; he said it would keep me from losing my phone but I never dreamed it would save my life. I'm so happy you found me when you did; I don't know how much longer I could've lasted. I feel exhausted."

"Do you feel up to going home with Tom? I want to be sure to arrest those two and see them behind bars. I'll need a full statement from you too but I'll swing by later for that."

"Oh my! Tom, the bag of nails I bought for you is still in that cabin. I guess my purse is there too along with the remains of my broken cell phone. Susan stomped on it," I recalled.

"I'll bring all that to you as soon as we capture those two. You go on home," Allen said.

"What about my truck? All the groceries are in it." Now that the danger was past, my mind turned to focus on chores left undone.

Tom laughed. "She's feeling better. Don't worry, I already drove the truck home. When Allen and I were searching earlier, I spotted the truck parked near Wiley's. I drove it home while Allen continued his investigation. As soon as Lionel told us the GPS location, I jumped in my own truck to get here to help search."

Taking a deep breath, I smiled at the two of them. "I should have known you would take care of everything. Let's go home. I need a long soak in a hot bath and one of your good meals."

"You got it, boss." Tom shook Allen's hand then led me to the clearing on the berm of the road where his truck and the police cruisers were parked.

I climbed into Tom's pickup and rested my head against the back of the seat. The realization of how close I came to dying made me shudder. Tom must have guessed my thoughts as he reached over to squeeze my hand and nodded.

Twenty minutes later, we pulled into the gravel yard in front of the inn with my welcoming committee. Luke barked and raced toward the truck and Prissy wound her body through my legs as I walked toward the steps and the wide veranda. As I climbed the steps, I saw Grannie pacing furiously back and forth above the porch. Her image glowed brightly against the night backdrop.

"Maddie-girl, you scared the wits out of me. Oh, I wish my spirit wasn't confined to this farm. I would have scared the life out of those felons if I'd been with you," Grannie declared. Her spectral image emitting a gust of icy air with her burst of emotion.

"Believe me, Grannie, for a while there I was afraid I'd be joining you in the afterlife. I've never been more frightened. I'm going to take a hot bath. I'll tell you all about what happened while I soak."

I trudged upstairs and Grannie floated after me. If Tom wondered who I had been speaking with on the porch, he never let on. Maybe he had an idea. I didn't plan on saying and I doubt he'd ever ask.

Chapter Eighteen

Golden Surprise

"Do you think there could be more Confederate money hidden here on the farm?" I asked Grannie as we relaxed on the porch swing. A whisper of a breeze caressed my skin as I toyed with my freshly shampooed hair. I sighed and breathed in the sweet scents of magnolia blossoms and meadow flowers. Above us, the moon glowed within a blanket of twinkling stars filling the night sky. In the distance, crickets chirped and tree frogs croaked their nocturnal music.

Grannie's image shimmered in the faint glow of porch lanterns as she floated above the swing. *"Why do you ask?"*

"It's just ... Susan Harding was so adamant about a treasure being here. Her assertion made me wonder if it could be true."

"I would have said no if you had asked me before finding that one coin, but now I'm not too sure. I'm trying to remember. It's been over sixty years since I first moved here. There was never any talk of such a thing, but still ..."

"You think it's a possibility, though. We looked inside that box, it had an old blanket and one coin. That's all."

"You need to look deeper," Grannie said as she vanished.

Good gracious, I wish she'd stop saying that. So cryptic. Where was I supposed to look deeper? I sat mulling her message and savoring the silence as Allen drove into the yard.

As he approached the steps, one foot on the bottom riser, Luke barked and trotted over to the detective. Allen paused to reward him with a scratch to the top of his large head and a pat on the back. The shepherd followed his every step as he joined me on the swing.

"Hey, how're you feeling? Is it too late for a visit?" He dropped my purse and the torn paper bag of nails onto the porch floor.

I pulled my light cotton robe around me, tying the loose belt as I scooted over to make room for him. Studying his face, I recognized the lines of worry and dark circles under his eyes from sleepless nights. His concern for me was etched on his features.

"You're always welcome, no matter the time. I'm okay; just glad to be home." I searched his face, trying to read his thoughts. "Is it over? Did you catch Susan and Carl?"

"Yeah, we got 'em. Once our men surrounded the cabin where they had returned, Carl gave up. He came out of the house with his hands raised. Susan refused. She dug in. We had to shoot tear gas into the cabin to drive her out. She finally stumbled outside, wiping her eyes and cursing us."

"Susan confessed to me that she shot Stanton Collier because he ruined her father's business and caused him to commit suicide. If she hadn't been holding a gun on me, I could have felt sorry for her. I don't think her brother had anything to do with Collier's shooting. However, Carl helped his sister by burying the pistol in the orchard," I said in a soft voice. I stared into the night, my mind reliving the horrors of my captivity.

"Don't feel too sorry for either of them. Remember, they hit your housekeeper on the head and tied her up in that tunnel, intending to leave her to die there."

Taking a deep breath, I turned to face Allen. "Does this mean you're releasing Sally? Clearly, she's innocent of the murder charges and she also wasn't involved in hunting for the treasure chest."

"Yes. The Chief approved releasing her from custody. Her only crime was unlocking the shed and allowing one of your guests to use a shovel. I don't think we can make any accessory charges stick."

"Good. I want her to come home to the inn. Seems like her only fault was believing James Warner and that's not a crime, just a mistake. How about James? Are you arresting him too?"

"Warner is being charged with attempted fraud. We've got him down at the station. He pleaded guilty to prowling around in the barn and knocking you over that night. He says he took off his muddy shoes and hid them in a suitcase. That's why we lost his tracks."

"Of course! Makes me feel so silly. I scrutinized everyone's feet when they checked out the next morning and couldn't figure out why no one had muddy shoes. But James Warner didn't check out; he stayed at the inn. He must have had plenty of time to clean the mud from those shoes. I don't know why I didn't think of it before."

"Don't be so hard on yourself, you've had a lot on your mind."

Allen picked up my hand and held it in his larger and warmer one. His thumb drew circles on the palm of my hand. We rocked silently, enjoying the night air. Luke curled at our feet and Prissy made herself comfortable on my lap as we moved gently back and forth.

I sighed, deciding to admit my earlier thoughts. "There have been so many twists and turns to this mess. You know, I'm still not convinced about the truth behind any missing gold."

"You think there are more hidden gold coins? Where?" Allen asked.

"I wish I knew. I'd like to get that old chest brought up from the basement where I can inspect it better in the light. I never got to examine it thoroughly."

"All right. No time like the present. Let's go get it," Allen said as he abruptly stood up, sending my swing careening.

"You're serious? Okay. Going down the basement during the dead of night isn't my favorite thing to do, but I guess I can muster up the courage. C'mon."

We entered the kitchen and headed to the basement door. Tom glanced up in surprise as we passed him. My dear friend and employee had insisted on staying with me until we learned the police had arrested that crazy Harding pair and they wouldn't be coming back to the inn to threaten us.

"What's going on? Does this mean you made an arrest?" Tom asked.

"Yes, he did. Right now, I want to carry up that strong hold box where we can get a better look at it," I said.

"Want some help?"

"It's okay. The box is empty, shouldn't be very heavy," I said.

"You stay here. I'll help bring it up," Tom insisted.

"Thanks. I've had enough close confinements for one day. Y'all can have at it," I said with a grateful smile as Tom and Allen stomped down the basement stairs.

I listened to the sounds of their movements. Their conversation was muted until Tom called out to me.

"This chest weighs a ton. I thought you said it was empty."

Leaning against the open doorway, I shouted into the deep basement. "It is. We left the key in the lock, check inside."

I heard more grunts and groans as the two men grasped the handles on the side of the chest and lugged it up the stairs. They were both panting when they gained the top step and kitchen floor.

"Don't tell me it took two strong men to carry one empty box? Are you guys kidding me?"

Allen made a big production of standing and straightening his kinked back. But he winked and smiled at his joke.

The chest sat in the middle of the kitchen floor, with the lid open. I kneeled down, sitting on my heels, and ran my hand around the inside of the empty box. I tapped the sides and bottom then sat back and stared at the chest.

"How deep is this box? Tom, grab your tape measure. I want to check the dimensions of this thing."

Tom held his ruler against the sides of the box. "Looks like about thirty inches wide by twenty across and maybe twenty inches deep."

"It can't be that deep. Measure inside from the edge of the lid to the bottom. Looks too shallow to be twenty inches," I said as I judged the dimensions of the chest before us.

"Maybe it's got a false bottom," suggested Allen

"That's got to be it!" Excitement built in me as I considered the possibilities. I recalled Grannie's words as she told me to look deeper. Did she mean deeper into the chest?

Tom grabbed a hammer from the toolbox he kept in the pantry. "How attached are you to this box? A couple strong whacks with this hammer ought to break it apart."

"Go ahead. Do it. I'm more interested to see what's in that false bottom," I said, clapping my hands.

Allen and Tom rolled the box onto its side then Tom raised the hammer and swung it against the wooden chest. It cracked but remained intact. Allen and I stood back and watched as Tom swung again, applying more force as he slammed the hammer into the wood. A loud crack sounded as the wood split and fell away.

Gold coins rolled out of the demolished box across the floor. The gold gleamed, sparkling under the bright kitchen lights.

I stood staring at the plunder, speechless. Looking at both Allen and Tom, their expressions mirrored my own sense of wonder.

"Holy cow! Well, that explains why that box weighed so much," Tom exclaimed. He picked up one of the coins and turned it over and over in the palm of his hand.

"Guess the rumors of Confederate gold were true. Good gracious, I can't believe it." I fingered one of the coins and read the inscription on the piece ... Confederate States of America, 1864. Wait until Lionel and Lily see this.

"What are you going to do with all this?" Allen asked as he too fingered a gold coin. "You can't keep it here, it's not safe."

I sat on one of the kitchen chairs and stared at the pile of gold. Allen was right. We'd be inviting all kinds of lookee-loos and thieves at the inn. I couldn't keep this. It wasn't really mine.

"You're right. How many coins are there? Let's count them. Tomorrow, I'll contact the UVA history department chairman. These belong in a museum," I said.

Tom and Allen made stacks of ten coins each, lined up in a row like little soldiers of the South. All total there were two hundred and five coins, including the first coin we had found. Impressive. I had no idea what the coins' value was. The weight of the gold bullion alone, priced in today's market value, had to be considerable.

I pressed one of the gold coins into Tom's hand. "You keep this. You've earned it, my friend. Save it for a rainy day or your retirement funds."

"Thanks, Maddie. That's real generous of you."

"Why don't you go home and get a good night's sleep. You must be exhausted after such a long day. Thanks for caring and staying with me too. I can always count on you, Tom," I said as I gave him a hug with tears glistening in my eyes.

"Where do you want these coins?" asked Allen.

Looking at the stack of coins on the floor, I thought of a heavy canvas bag used for marketing stored in the pantry. I opened the pantry and rummaged through a collection of cloth shopping bags until I found the heavy canvas bag.

"This should hold them. It's pretty sturdy. Let's scoop them up and put the gold in this then I'll lock it in my office until I contact the history department and museum."

It was close to midnight when Allen finally left and I sat alone with Grannie in the moonlight.

"I never would have believed Magnolia Blossom contained hidden Confederate gold if I hadn't seen it with my own eyes. Charlie's father had

hinted about the farm being involved in some raid during the war and a refuge for Confederate generals. I suppose those gold coins must be part of that," Grannie said.

Her words made me realize the Brooke family and Magnolia Blossom had a role in our nation's history. I had no doubt now that the newly discovered gold belonged in a museum, safe and sound and out of temptation of future treasure hunters.

Chapter Nineteen

Vows

The late morning light streamed through the windows of the Magnolia Blossom Inn, casting a warm, golden glow over the sitting room. My heart swelled with a mixture of relief and joy as I took in the scene before me—Savannah and Stephen, arm in arm, smiling at each other in a way that only two people deeply in love could.

"Oh Grannie, I'm so glad things turned out okay," I whispered.

"You did the right thing, sugar ... donating that gold to the American Civil War Museum. Those coins only brought trouble to this place, best to get rid of them."

"If anything was cursed, I feel like it was that cache of coins. I am glad to be rid of them. Besides, the museum paid us a tidy finder's fee, so it wasn't a total loss."

"You were very gracious to let those kids come back and get married here too. I'm looking forward to watching the ceremony. Maybe one day it will be yours," Grannie said with a chuckle as she vanished above the porch roof.

Luke barked and jumped up and down, trying to catch her image as she floated away like a soap bubble.

"Can you believe it?" Savannah asked as she walked up the veranda steps, turning to me with a radiant grin. "After everything that's happened, we're finally getting married. And here, at your beautiful inn like we had planned."

I smiled back, smoothing down the front of my pale lavender gown, the one I'd chosen for my new role as her maid of honor. "I'm just glad you two worked things out. It means a lot to me that Magnolia Blossom Inn can host your special day."

Savannah smiled wistfully, her eyes misting over as she glanced at Stephen. "Thank you for agreeing to be in our wedding. You caught my father's killer. I owe you my gratitude for seeing justice done." She gazed into the cloudless sky as she sought to put her feelings into words. "I'll never forgive myself for bringing that woman into our lives. I'm just sorry my Daddy can't be here."

I gave her a hug and said in a soft voice, "He's here. He's here in your heart."

She nodded and pressed her fingertips to stop a tear threatening to drop.

It was hard to believe how much had changed in such a short amount of time. Just a few weeks ago, the chaos surrounding Stanton Collier's murder and the hunt for hidden treasure had consumed the entire town. And now, here we were, preparing for a wedding—a small, intimate ceremony of just family and close friends, the way it should be.

Susan Harper—Harding, I reminded myself—was behind bars, where she belonged. Her desperate scheme for revenge had unraveled, and the truth had finally come to light. It was tragic what had happened to her family, but murder was never the answer. The law had dealt with her and her brother, Carl. I couldn't help but feel a sense of closure, knowing that justice had been served.

And James Warner, who'd had his own secrets, was also facing the consequences of his actions. Allen had arrested him for fraud, which was why Stephen had asked his cousin to step in as his best man. It was an unexpected twist, but one that felt right.

My gaze drifted over to Allen, who was standing near the veranda, talking quietly with Tom. He was dressed in a dark black suit, his hair neatly combed and beard trimmed. For a moment, I forgot to breathe. There was something about seeing him in that suit, with the weight of the investigation lifted, that made my heart skip a beat.

"Looking good, Yankee," I called out, unable to resist teasing him.

He turned toward me, a slow grin spreading across his face. "You're not looking so bad yourself, Maddie."

I rolled my eyes, but I couldn't suppress the warmth that blossomed in my chest at the way he was looking at me. There had always been this unspoken tension between us—something that went beyond the frustrating arguments and the moments when he pushed me harder than anyone else. I had learned that his protective streak came from something deeper—a tragedy in his past that had shaped him into the man he was today.

Now, though, there was no mistaking the shift in the air between us. It was softer, less guarded.

"Can we get started?" Stephen's voice broke through the moment, and I blinked, realizing that the time had come.

The wedding ceremony was to be held on the front lawn under the newly formed flower archway, with the sprawling magnolia trees framing the scene. Chairs were arranged along the front walk. A white runner ran down the center surrounded by a gay scattering of flower petals decorating the aisle. The noon sun was just beginning to filter through the branches in the most picturesque way. I had decorated the barn with cheerful flowers in Savannah's pink and lavender colors, including an intimate arrangement of dining tables for the reception. Tom spent the day before preparing a wedding feast the couple would long remember. We wanted this special day to replace any tragic memories from before.

Savannah tugged on my arm as the music started, her smile wide and nervous all at once. "You ready?"

"Absolutely," I said, squeezing her hand. "Let's do this."

I handed her the bridal bouquet of white and pink roses surrounded by baby's breath and delicate fern fronds. Stepping behind her, I straightened her gown's train and smoothed the gossamer veil around her shoulders.

"You look lovely," I told Savannah as I picked up my own nosegay of lavender and pink rosebuds.

I walked ahead of her down the aisle, taking my place across from Stephen and trying not to focus too much on the fact that Allen was standing beside him just a few feet away. His eyes found mine as I took my position, and a current of electricity zipped through me, making my pulse quicken. I couldn't help but feel that there was something unspoken between us, something that might finally find its way to the surface.

Hugh and Beatrice Beauregard sat in the front row. I wondered if Hugh regretted the bride would bring no dowery like old Southern custom formerly dictated. He had counted on getting his hands on the Collier money to resolve his gambling debts. Perhaps his son would float him a loan.

Martha Collier stepped forward to accompany her daughter and to give her away. Her face wore a sad smile, no doubt thinking of her husband's absence in their daughter's nuptials.

Savannah, her arm linked with her mother's, floated down the aisle moments later, looking every bit the radiant bride. Stephen's face lit up as she approached, and for a moment, the rest of the world faded away, leaving only the two of them connected in a way that was truly beautiful.

The ceremony was short but sweet, filled with heartfelt vows and quiet smiles shared between family members. When it came time for Stephen to place the ring on Savannah's finger, I saw him glance at Allen, a silent nod of gratitude passing between them.

Allen, standing in as best man, looked completely at ease in the role. He handed over the ring with a small smile. For a fleeting moment, I wondered what it would be like to be in Savannah's shoes—standing there with someone I loved, making promises for the future.

The ceremony concluded with the soft sound of applause, and as Savannah and Stephen shared their first kiss as husband and wife, a sense of peace settled over me.

"Well," I said as I stepped over to Allen after the ceremony, a playful smile tugging at my lips. "Looks like you're getting pretty good at this whole wedding thing. Maybe you should stick around."

Allen chuckled, but his gaze was more serious than his tone. "Maybe I will."

There was a pause, the air between us thick with possibility. I wasn't sure if it was the atmosphere of the wedding or the fact that we'd both been through so much together, but something had shifted. I could feel it in the way his eyes lingered on mine, in the way he seemed to stand just a little closer than usual.

"Thanks for standing up for Stephen," I said, my voice softer now. "I know it meant a lot to him."

"I'd do anything for family," he replied, his eyes never leaving mine.

"And for me?" I asked, the words slipping out before I could stop them.

Allen's expression softened, a warmth creeping into his gaze that made my heart race. "I'd do anything for you, Maddie."

The words hung in the air between us, and for a moment, I wasn't sure what to say. But then Allen took a step closer, his hand brushing against mine, and I realized that maybe I didn't need to say anything at all.

The wedding reception spilled out from the barn onto the lawn, where guests mingled and laughed, celebrating the newlyweds. Savannah and Stephen danced beneath the magnolia trees. The light of the setting sun cast a golden glow over the scene.

"Come on," Allen said, offering his hand to me with a crooked smile. "Dance with me."

I hesitated for just a second, but then I placed my hand in his, letting him lead me onto the dance floor. The music was soft and slow, and as Allen pulled me into his arms, the rest of the world seemed to fade away.

I rested my head against his chest, feeling the steady rhythm of his heartbeat beneath my cheek.

Grannie hovered above, her spectral image swaying to the music, and smiled down on us. I raised my eyes to her, and she nodded.

"This is what I wanted for you, Maddie-girl. He's a good man."

For the first time in what felt like forever, everything was calm. The chaos of the last few weeks had passed, and now, standing here in Allen's arms, I couldn't help but think that maybe—just maybe—I'd found exactly where I was meant to be.

"So," I murmured, looking up at him as we swayed to the music. "What happens next?"

Allen's smile was slow, his eyes filled with a warmth that made my chest tighten. "I guess that's up to us, isn't it?"

I nodded, a smile tugging at my lips as I leaned in a little closer. "Yes suh, I guess it is," I said in my deepest Southern drawl.

Author Biography

An avid reader since childhood, Nancy M. Wade always enjoyed writing stories and upon formal retirement in 2012, she decided to pursue her passion formally.

Nancy has written five historical novels, including a western action adventure trilogy called the "Circle-D Saga".

A lover of all things mysterious, Nancy created two cozy mystery series. "A Meadowood Mystery" is set in a small Ohioan town with amateur sleuth and housewife, Meredith Gardner. There are six novels to date in this series.

The "Maddie Brooke Mystery" series includes two novels centered in a historic, southern bed and breakfast inn where recent college graduate turned sleuth, Maddie Brooke, resides with her German shepherd, Luke, and her grandmother's spirited ghost.

Nancy is a member of the Tri-Cities Lost State Writers Guild and is an honors graduate of East Tennessee State University.

You can follow her author pages on Instagram and Facebook or her web site at: https://nancymwadeauthor.com .

Excerpt: Innvitation to Murder
A Maddie Brooke Mystery

Welcome to "Innvitation to Murder," a captivating cozy mystery set at the picturesque Magnolia Blossom Inn, nestled in the charming town of Clarkstown at the gateway to the Shenandoah Valley and Blue Ridge Mountains just outside Charlottesville, VA.

Meet Maddie Brooke, recent graduate of UVA Charlottesville, and a young woman who unexpectedly inherits the inn from her late grandmother, Polly Brooke. With the support of her best friends: computer wizard Lionel Hogan and intern physician Lily Chung, Maddie sets out to breathe new life into the inn and honor her grandmother's legacy while investigating her grandmother's sudden death.

However, tranquility quickly turns to turmoil when a college student is murdered during his stay at the inn. Handsome, Yankee police detective Allen Crawford arrives to investigate, and sparks fly between him and Maddie as they work together to unravel the mystery.

As Maddie delves deeper into the two deaths, she discovers secrets that lead back to her own family history. To complicate matters, Grannie's ghost makes occasional appearances at the inn, offering cryptic clues and adding an otherworldly twist to the investigation.

Amidst the chaos, Maddie's cousin, Bobbie Jo Taylor, arrives and proves to be a mischievous troublemaker, stirring up drama and suspicion at every turn.

With twists, turns, and a touch of romance, "Innvitation to Murder" is a delightful blend of intrigue, friendship, and small-town charm that will keep readers guessing until the very end.

www.ingramcontent.com/pod-product-compliance
Lightning Source LLC
Chambersburg PA
CBHW071128100726
47908CB00008B/2525